"Yelena"

A story of unmitigated Love and Passion.

Jac. K. Spence

iUniverse LLC
Bloomington

"YELENA" A STORY OF UNMITIGATED LOVE AND PASSION.

iUniverse books may be ordered through booksellers or by contacting:

iUniverse
1663 Liberty Drive
Bloomington, IN 47403
www.iuniverse.com
1-800-Authors (1-800-288-4677)

ISBN: 978-1-4917-2484-2 (sc)
ISBN: 978-1-4917-2485-9 (e)

Printed in the United States of America.

iUniverse rev. date: 02/12/2014

An Autumn Affair

It was the autumn of 1982 when Bill Bond decided to take square dance lessons at the local county recreation facility. His wife, Betsy Bond, was on a two month tour of Europe with several of her best friends from her Woman's Club. It just happened that the wife of Pravda's Washington bureau chief, Fedora Volkova, was also enrolled wanting to learn as much as possible about American folk dancing prior to their return to Russia. Her husband, Georgy Volkov, would drive her to class but did not participate claiming to be too clumsy with his feet.

It was an eight week course with two 90 minute classes per week. The participants were mostly married couples and since Bill Bond and Fedora Volkova were without their spouses they became dancing partners. On the fourth week of classes, Fedora's sister Galina, arrived from Russia for a multi-week visit and she would come to the studio with her sister and brother-in-law and be an observer. She was beautiful beyond words and when the three of them invited Bill to go to a pub close by after class, for a cocktail, he accepted their invitation without giving it much thought. Bill left his car at the studio parking lot and sat up front with Georgy while the two sisters sat in the back.

It was a fun evening talking about many common things concerning their respective countries, even extending their conversation to politics and their respective presidents, Mikhail Gorbachev and Ronald Reagan. On the way back to Bill's car Georgy suggested that Bill and Galina sit in the back because no doubt he had noticed that they were bonding. Almost without thinking Bill extended his hand toward hers and within a minute they were clenching tightly. There was little doubt that there was a special magic in the air and when Bill drove home that evening he understood he had been smitten by this Russian beauty. He could not erase the thought that he wanted to share time with her in some intimate setting.

Bill's 22 year marriage to Betsy Bond was a good one and although there was some rough times they were always able to settle any misunderstandings in an amicable way. On subsequent evenings, after dance class, Georgy suggested that maybe Bill might want to take Galina out to dinner sometime, without him and Fedora. He had no doubt recognized that they had become very fond of each other and wanted Bill to know they had no objections.

So, one evening as they exited class, Bill summoned the courage to ask Galina to join him for dinner and she accepted thanking him for the invitation. Bill wanted to try the new Polynesian Restaurant at the Marriott hotel complex just off the beltway in Bethesda, Maryland. They both agreed the food and service was terrific and as he drove her to the Volkov residence in Silver Spring they both understood they wanted more time together before her return to Russia. As he walked her to the door, they ended their evening with a spontaneous hug and meaningful kiss. It was obvious that they both wanted to extend this moment to some future time when they could express their fondness in a more expansive way.

Knowing that Galina was trying to forget some unfortunate experience back home both Georgy and Fedora were so happy that Galina was getting a sort of therapy that she was badly in need of. So, when Bill invited her to dinner again, she expressed a desire to go back to the Polynesian Restaurant, saying she had not only enjoyed their offerings, but with the island furniture and music it created a most romantic ambiance.

When she spoke the words, "romantic ambiance" Bill interpreted it to mean that it was now time for him to take the initiative, so, since she had several more weeks before returning to Russia he decided to take the special offer that Marriott was offering on their honeymoon suite. Rent for one week and the second week was half price. As their dinner was ending he told her what he had done. She took his hand and whispered, "I can't wait, can we start tonight?" With that, she called her sister and Georgy and let them know not to worry if she got in extra late tonight. After talking to them in Russian, she continued with her earlier thought, "Yes Bill, I want to make love to you tonight because you have filled my life with happiness since my arrival here. I have not asked you about your marital status and I do not want to know. Likewise, you have not inquired about my life in Russia, and I appreciate that because the last several years have not been pleasant for me."

She continued, "My sister and brother-in-law encouraged my friendship with you because they understood I needed to purge my mind of my negative thoughts. Now let us go to the suite you have reserved and hopefully what we give each other will give us good memories long after we have parted."

Needless to say, Bill was excited with her overture, and the experiences he enjoyed with her that evening and the ones that followed prior to her return to Russia was unforgettable. They exchanged messages over the next year or so but when she told Bill she had met a wonderful man by the name of Vitali Sokolov he understood it was time to end all communication between them.

Also, Betsy Bond had returned from Europe and was back in his life in a big way and their marriage was going well. So, maybe the time Bill and Galina spent together over those special autumn nights in 1982 turned out best for both. But now it was 2026 and Bill Bond had passed away over a year ago. When he met Galina she was 27 and now she was 71.

Bill and Betsy Bond had an amicable separation after nearly four decades and now in the autumn of his years he began a friendship with another young Russian woman by the name of Olga Kornakova and from 2010 until his death in the spring of 2025 they had experienced so much together including a few romantic interludes. In that same time frame, Olga married a CIA operative by the name of Ben Stevens, and they had two daughters by the name of Marina and Anastasia. Their marriage had been strained when Olga learned that Ben had a mistress and during that time she sought the company of Bill for comfort and solace in those trying days. By 2026 Ben had given up his mistress and their marriage was on a tenuous mend.

They were living in Easton, Maryland at the time when Olga received this letter:

"Dear Ms. Kornakova, You don't know me but my name is Vasily Sokolov. My mother's name is Galina Sokolova and she is now residing in a hospital here in Russia and her health providers tell me she has just several months to live. Recently, she has given me some news that I could hardly believe, and I am having a difficult time dealing with it. I had always assumed my biological father was Vitali Sokolov who passed away 2 years ago this month. My mother told me when she visited America in September of 1982 she had a brief two week intimate relationship with a man by the name of Bill Bond. When she arrived back in Russia several months later she learned she was pregnant. Yes, you guessed right, Bill Bond is my father. I have no doubt about this but I want to learn more. She asked me to contact you since she remembered you and Bill Bond had a lot of notoriety during the spy exchange program over a decade ago."

"I love Russia and have a good position here in Yaroslavi as Administrator of Roads and Bridges. My mother left the USA in late October of 1982 and my birth date was July 25th 1983. My objective is to obtain dual citizenship because of all the advantages it infers. Is there any way you could help me in this matter? Respectfully Yours, Vasily Sokolov"

Olga could hardly believe what she just read. The implications were enormous and immediately she thought of the bra she had been keeping in one of her storage boxes which contained the sperm of Bill Bond. It would be an easy DNA sample for Vasily but how could she explain this to Ben and for that matter to Vasily. Olga thought it strange that during all the years she knew Bill Bond from the summer of 2010 to the time of his death in the spring of 2025 he had never mentioned his affair with Galina Sokolova in 1982. His return e-mail address was on his letterhead so she decided to respond.

"Dear Mr. Sokolov I may be able to help you but I will need some time to think things over. I calculate you will be 43 this year so you are young enough to wait a little. I will hit that magic 40 year mark on Nov. 1 of this year. Regards, Olga."

She immediately went to her favorite Russian search engine and put in this information: "Photographs of government officials in Yaroslavi, Russian Federation." OMG! there he was and there was little doubt that his father was Bill Bond. Maybe she could send a picture to the immigration authorities of Bill Bond gazing down the Volga River that she had taken of him while visiting Kostroma in May of 2011. Of course she was smart enough to know that comparing pictures would not be sufficient enough to prove anything.

It was now March and Ben had been encouraging her for some time to take their daughters to Russia to visit their maternal grandparents and now maybe this would be the time. So, in her mind, she circled the months of June and July and maybe she would stay there the entire two months. This would be an opportunity for Ben to live the life of a single man over this period of time without wife or mistress to test his sincerity.

Of course she would not be honest with herself if she didn't admit that Vasily Sokolov provided the impetus for her planned visit. Also, for quite some time, she wanted to visit her parents and for Marina and Anastasia to see their grandparents after so many years would be a real treat for everyone.

Within the hour after sending her response to Vasily regarding his letter she got this return e-mail: "Thanks so much for responding to my letter. I look forward to continuing our dialog hoping I can have some resolution to my situation. By the way, my mother never told Bill Bond she was carrying his baby. She was not sure about his marital status at the time and thought it best to keep it from him. In fact, my mother met Vitali shortly after she learned she was pregnant, and neither gave any hint through all those years that I was not Vitali's biological son, until my mum broke the news just a few weeks ago. With highest regards, Vasily Sokolov."

Olga decided not to tell him she found his photo on the Russian search engine leaving little doubt in her mind that Vasily was the biological son of Bill Bond. But now, her curiosity was running at breakneck speed. Was he married? Did he have children? Of course, it was way too early to make these kinds of personal inquiries, but now just meeting him would be one of her top priorities. She decided not to tell Ben anything about her communication with Vasily or her planned trip to Russia to visit him and her parents until he returned from his temporary assignment in Honolulu in several weeks.

Olga had mentioned the possibility to her two girls in the past, that she would be taking them to Russia one day to visit their grandparents and they seemed anxious to go. When they returned home from school today she would break the news. Her mind was filled with a thousand thoughts and she began to wonder what Bill Bond would have done if he knew he had a son in Russia. It was just over a year ago she mixed his ashes with the two pints of soil, as he requested, and climbed the hill at Chincoteague, and dispersed his remains behind the old lighthouse. It seemed almost unfair that he did not learn a few years earlier about Vasily. But now, it was all about planning for the coming trip. She could not wait to see Vasily in person. Was he really as handsome as he appeared in his picture? Did he inherit his dad's irrepressible personality? Bill had a knack for flirting with beautiful women, so she could only imagine that Vasily's mum had to be very special.

Olga had never mentioned to Ben about her relationship with Bill Bond over the past few years of his life, and if she decided to give up her bra with Bill's semen to assure Vasily of the dual citizenship he sought, it would be a bridge she would cross later. Of course, during that period of time, Ben was still seeing his mistress. And how would she explain to Vasily the circumstances surrounding her intimacy with his father Bill Bond, while still being married to Ben Stevens? All of this would have to be sorted out in the future but for now it was time to think about her impending trip.

The girls were now home from school and when she told them of her plans to take them to Russia they were excited and happy. She called her mum, Marina, in Kostroma and she almost burst into tears because she and Andrey had been preparing for this visit for many years, and now finally, they would be seeing their granddaughters. Olga decided not to wait until Ben returned and instead she called him in Honolulu. Although it took him by complete surprise, he told her it was good that she was doing this since her parents would enjoy it more while they were both in good health.

When Bill passed away he left most of his assets to Betsy Bond and she needed the money since her medical bills were sizable but he was kind enough to also bequeath a nice amount to Olga, and she would now use some of it to finance their trip. They would be spending June and July there and so they could pack lightly. She had a friend Inna, living in Kostroma, who was a dressmaker, and decided to wait until they arrived in Kostroma where she and her two girls could get fitted for summer dresses.

When Ben got home from Honolulu, he was the perfect dad and husband taking the three of them to either Ocean City or Rehoboth Beach every nice weekend during April and May, to ride the bikes or fly kites or just walk on the beach. Going to Grotto's for pizza and pasta was one of their favorite places, and taking the ferry across Delaware Bay to have lunch at one of the sidewalk cafes at Cape May was a special treat.

But now May 31st had arrived and it was time to pack Ben's van, because in the morning, they would be driving to the Dulles International Airport for the flight to Moscow, where Olga's father, Andrey, would be waiting to take them to Kostroma. They would be taking the Russian Airline Aeroflot and it would be a direct 13 hour flight. The next day Ben left Olga and the girls off on the platform at the terminal building where they exchanged hugs and kisses. Ben then proceeded on to Langley for an afternoon meeting with the director. Olga decided not to mention Vasily Sokolov, or his letter to Ben, thinking it might upset him at a time when they were having such a great time together as a family. But there was little doubt that Vasily was on her mind as their plane lifted off the runway.

For the first week of their visit, Olga would not e-mail Vasily, deciding to give full attention to her family and friends in Kostroma. She could not allow the affection she had for Bill Bond to spill over to his son. Olga's mind shifted back to her last year in high school when she was recruited by the RIS after a strong recommendation from her primary instructor. She was elated to be chosen and when she went to the Russian Intelligence Service Training Academy at Yasenevo she excelled. She gladly and proudly signed the so called 3B pledge which was short hand to be willing to use your brains, beauty and body to accomplish your mission.

And at age 22 she was sent to Delmarva to begin her first assignment. Her objective was to get a job as a server or hostess at one or more restaurants, find a good candidate for a cover, and then set up her transponder and transmitters on the beach at Chincoteague. These devices were already being produced in the RIS secret underground laboratory in Norfolk, Virginia. When she first arrived in Delmarva in the spring of 2009 it took her to the summer of 2010 to find the perfect candidate to be her cover for her clandestine activities and his name was Bill Bond.

That was long ago, and her days in the RIS ended in 2013 when she turned herself in to American authorities in Moscow. But now, it was 2026, and Olga and her girls were approaching Moscow, and soon they would be on the ground. Since their luggage was sparse they cleared security and customs quickly, and her father, Andrey, was waiting in the reception area. It was a glorious mini-reunion as they walked toward his van for the five hour trip to Kostroma. Thankfully, Olga had taught her daughters the Russian language and while at home she spoke to them quite often in Russian so conversing with their grandfather was not a problem.

When they arrived in Kostroma, her mother, Marina, was there to greet them. For the rest of the day and the entire first week it was all about family and friends. They would visit all the places that Olga remembered growing up as a child and young adult like schools, church, sporting venues and even places where she met her first boyfriends.

Olga, along with her daughter`s Marina and Anastasia went by to get fitted for their traditional Russian summer dresses which Inna promised to have ready in about a week.

Although she had talked to Ben a few times on the phone since she arrived, she wanted to remind him of a few chores he would need to think about, since normally they would be things she would do if she were home so she penned him an e-mail: "Dear Ben, we are enjoying ourselves immensely and the girls are out with their grandparents having lunch at McDonalds of all places, and yes it is a very popular venue here too. Don`t forget to put the trash out on Tuesday mornings, and be sure to bring in the mail and pay all the bills by the 25th so they will arrive by the first. Also, when you depart for work don`t forget to turn the thermostat up to 82 degrees because electricity is very expensive. Miss you a lot. Love, Olga"

Now it was time to write to Vasily. She had written to him before leaving the USA that she would send him an e-mail about a week after arriving in Russia. She understood she would need to choose her words carefully so she sat down and sent him this message:

A Meeting, A Massage, A Confession

"Hi Vasily, I hope all is going well in your life. We arrived in Kostroma about a week ago and are enjoying ourselves very much. If you have any time for lunch one day I will be happy to meet you. Maybe some place between here and Yaroslavi would be o.k. with me. Just to let you know, my parents will be taking my daughters to their dacha for a taste of Russian country living, between the 11th and 15th of this month and any of those days would be best for me. Olga"

Within the hour he responded: "Dear Olga, I can't adequately express how much your letter meant to me. Can we meet for lunch at the Romanov Forest Ecotel on the 11th at 11:45 a.m. at the entrance of the main dining room?" Many thanks, Vasily}

Her response: "Yes, I will be looking forward to meeting you."

When the morning of the 11th arrived Olga and her parents were up early. Marina and Andrey were packing their van for the four day trip to their dacha which was about 250 kilometers from Kostroma. Taking their grandchildren to their little piece of paradise reminded them of the time they would take Olga when she was growing up. This was a big day for Olga because she was to meet Vasily Sokolov for lunch, and although she didn't tell her parents about her impending engagement, they had noticed she was particularly upbeat and happy. They attributed her mood to getting a break after a week of meeting friends and family members.

It was 9a.m when Olga's parents and daughters got on their way for their mini-vacation at their dacha and she would need to be at the

Ecotel by 11:45. When she first arrived in Kostroma she made a good deal for a car rental for the two months she would be here. It would be a 25 minute drive so she would need to do some quick chores and then get her shower and do her makeup. This was the day she would pick up the summer dresses she had ordered from Inna. She chose to wear a white one piece dress. Before she got in her car for her meeting with Vasily, a neighbor remarked that Olga looked more beautiful than she could ever remember. It was now 11:15 as she began the drive toward the Romanov Forest.

On her way there, she remembered 15 years earlier of driving to the same place with Bill Bond and her good friend, Anthony. It was Vasily who suggested they meet there and although she suggested meeting somewhere about half way between Kostroma and Yaroslavi his drive time would be longer than hers. That, by itself, reminded her of Bill Bond who was always looking to make it easier for the other person. Of course, the Romanov Forest complex was a special place, and perhaps his intent was more for the ambiance than who had the longest drive. As she drove into the parking lot, there was a man standing on the pathway and there was little doubt this was Vasily. The facial characteristics were unmistakable. Without a doubt, this was the son of Bill Bond.

As she got out of her car and walked toward him they embraced as if they were high school sweethearts who had not seen each other for several decades. As they walked in the direction of the restaurant he was the first to speak, "My mother told me of your beauty but you exceeded all my expectations." She countered with this, "It is sad that Bill Bond did not know he had a son in Russia. He would have been so proud."

While dining she told Vasily how proud he would have been of his father. "I don't blame your mother for being smitten by him because even in the autumn of his years he was quite the charmer." Vasily explained that when his mother visited America in 1982 she went there to escape a bad situation at home and when she returned and learned she was pregnant she was really happy. Not long after she met Vitali, she said he had a similar personality as Bill. After a year of dating and about 18 months after my birth she married Vitali.

11

"I want you to know that Vitali was a good man and I have nothing but fond memories of him. Just because I want to learn more about my biological father in no way diminishes the way I feel about him. He treated me well and made sure I got a good education. Now Olga, tell me a little about you."

She explained that she was happily married with two daughters who were with her here in Russia but decided not to mention what happened when Ben was seeing his mistress, while she going to Chincoteague on occasion to be with Bill Bond. She told him of her days in the Russian Intelligence Service and her mission in America and how and when she first met his father.

After their steak and salmon dinner they decided to walk the grounds of this historic and natural reserve. The cottages they had constructed among the trees were done in such a way as if they were part of the forest itself. "Now Vasily I don`t want to make you feel uncomfortable but since I knew your father so well I would love to know as much as you can tell me about your life in Russia." He responded in this way, "I don`t want to bore you so I will keep it as short as possible."

"I will leave my early life out for now but when I was 27 I met a 21 year old woman by the name of Magdalina Brezhneva who was in her third year of medical school. We were married within six months after we met. I had graduated from the Moscow State University of Civil Engineering four years earlier and got a decent job as a planner in the Moscow office of Roads and Bridges. I wanted to have children right away but she wanted to wait until she earned all her degrees and licenses and established a reputation in the field of gynecology."

"After 10 years with no children they decided it would be best to separate. She had completed several internships at major Moscow hospitals and established an impeccable reputation. She eventually moved to St. Petersburg and established her own practice which I understand is doing very well. I wanted to get away from Moscow and when I was offered the job as Administrator of Roads and Bridges in Yaroslavi, I took the job without thinking twice about it. The salary was excellent and I loved the challenge because Yaroslavi is an old city and much had to be done to its infrastructure. That was five years ago and although there is plenty left to do the improvements are beginning to make a difference. So that is my life in a nutshell from age 27 until now when I will turn 43 in a little over a month." As they walked back to the hotel complex Olga knew that Vasily was someone special and wondered how his first wife Magdalina ever allowed him to get away. "Did your wife ever re-marry?"

"No as a matter of fact our divorce was not finalized until last year."

When they entered the lobby of the Ecotel neither wanted the day to end so they walked around to see what other services were offered. As they passed the room where a woman was getting a massage, Olga remarked that one day, before returning to the USA, she would come back here to use their pool and get a massage.

Whether Vasily thought this was an opening or not only he knew when he decided to reveal a little more about his personal life with Magdalina Brezhneva.

"Our marriage was far from perfect but the one thing she enjoyed most was getting a massage so I learned to be the perfect masseur. When I say perfect I am only joking but I did take a course to improve my skills. So, at least once a week, I would give her this service and she would reciprocate. Sometimes I think it was the thing that kept our marriage together as long as it did."

There was little doubt this revelation affected Olga in a very personal way as her complexion turned reddish and she could not find the words to respond when all of a sudden she managed a smile and then she looked him right in the eye.

"Would you consider doing that service for me?" Without hesitation he responded, "I would be honored to do so and since all government officials get a special rate I will get a cabin with two entry cards. You can go there and look it over while I gather some supplies."

She understood the implications if Ben discovered she received a massage in a private cabin being administered by the biological son of Bill Bond. Her parents would not look kindly on it either. But Olga could not resist his offer because she was now under his spell.

After getting the key to cabin #8 she went there to wait for Vasily. She removed her clothes and took a quick shower and then covered herself with a lush towel and sat on the edge of the bed. Soon she heard the electronic key in the door and he entered with a big smile holding several sheets and a good size bottle of oil.

"You need to have nice memories while here in Russia and this will only enhance our fantastic day." He began to spread the sheets on the carpeted floor and then he continued, "I will take a shower and then if you don't mind I will remain in the nude while administering the oil and trust me it will make the entire experience more exciting and enjoyable." By this time she could not resist his offer even if she tried because this is something she wanted so badly. "You won't need the towel around you but if you give it to me I will make a pillow for you."

Now they were both in the nude and as she lay down he remarked that she reminded him of Aphrodite, The Goddess of Love. She remembered that his father Bill Bond had made that same comparison just prior to their time in bed at Chincoteague after the great storm that almost ended their lives. He put on a pair of gloves that reminded her of the same material they use for condoms, and as he began to pour on the oil to her navel and breasts using a slow circular movement of his hands to all those areas. Then, gently spreading her legs, leaning down to kiss her vulva before applying the oil and continuing his slow hand motion.

It was now time to turn her over repeating everything he had done to her front side giving equal treatment to the cheeks, back thighs, as well as her shoulders and neck. He could not resist kissing and using his tongue on her most sensitive places prior to applying the oil. She now understood how lucky she was, because it is an experience every woman should have, and to think his ex-wife was getting this service every week made her envious of a woman she didn't know.

He turned her over again telling her the front side always gets more attention. This time his hand began to move to the area of the vulva when he asked, "Can I go inside?"..... "Yes, please do, but only if you remove your gloves, I like the feel of bare hands in that part."

After a few minutes she let out a shriek of pure joy and it was obvious that she had a powerful orgasm. In fact, the rush of blood to that area of her body made her slip into a brief moment of sleep almost acting as a sedative. When she came out of her slumber she insisted on returning the favor for Vasily. She used the remaining portion of oil on his most sensitive parts and when he had a full release he apologized for taking advantage of a situation where he lost complete control.

"I wanted it to happen and had you not taken it where you did I would have been highly disappointed, and would have wondered if I had lost all my appeal. I can't properly express how happy you made me today and I shall never forget it."

With that, they took a shower together and wrapped up the sheets and it was now 7p.m. Their 12 o'clock luncheon turned out to be a seven hour extravaganza and as they walked to the parking lot they promised to get together again in some venue over the next several months. Not necessarily to repeat what happened today but just be together because it was obvious to both they cared for each other. Vasily never asked her about how she could help him obtain dual citizenship but after what happened in the cabin today, when the right moment arrived to tell him about Bill Bond's sperm on her bra she would be more comfortable with discussing the circumstances about that night in Chincoteague.

As she drove back home to Kostroma her mind could only think of Vasily Sokolov. She would need to call her parents when she got home to see how their day went at the dacha. When she arrived home and got out of her car the same neighbor who remarked how beautiful she was when she departed earlier today said she looked even more beautiful now. When she got inside the house, she called her mum, and after hearing her daughter's voices in the background, she could tell they were having a good time. Grandpa was in the middle of teaching them the fine art of chess.

She told her mum she had spent a good portion of the day at the Romanoff Forest having lunch and then having a nice swim after which she jogged a few miles. Olga decided to wait until tomorrow to talk to her daughters because she really needed the rest. She did not mention

Vasily to her mother and would keep her secret as long as possible. She tossed and turned most of the night thinking only of Vasily Sokolov. Had she already fallen in love after spending just seven hours with him?

When she did awake it was already 10am and the first thing she did was call her parents and talk to her daughters. Some of the vegetables like cabbage, carrots, onions and leeks were ready to be harvested so today their project was to make a huge pot of Russian cabbage soup. Since most of the soup would go into glass jars the girls would also get a lesson in the "canning process." In the modern world this had become a lost art. After her conversation with Marina and Anastasia she checked her e-mails and received this one from Vasily.

"Dear Olga, I hope you don't mind me calling you by your first name. I hardly slept last night because you were constantly on my mind. I pray you won't think less of me because of what happened yesterday. I was overwhelmed by your beauty and I guess I was trying to show off my skills as an amateur masseur. When you expressed a desire to come back to the hotel at some time in the future to get a massage from the house masseur I guess I considered it an opening to tell you about how I use to perform the service for my ex-wife." I also wanted to tell you that when my Russian father, Vitali passed away two years ago I got a first floor flat for my mother here in Yaroslavi. You may remember when I first wrote you I told you she was in the hospital and only had several months to live. Now I have been told she has only several weeks. So, I will need to visit her on a daily basis and will need to stay close to the city. If you can write me to let me know you are not angry with me it will really lift my spirit. Vasily"

Almost immediately she sent back this e-mail, "Dear Vasily, I am most happy we are now on a first name basis. What happened yesterday will always be a cherished memory for me. I made it happen because I wanted it to happen. I am so sorry to hear about your mother. I want to meet her so badly. Is it possible I could visit you after your work tomorrow? There is so much I want to talk to you about concerning your dual citizenship and maybe you would be kind enough to take me to the hospital to meet your mum. Tomorrow is best for me because I want to see you before my parents and daughters return from the dacha. I can leave here about 3p.m and be in Yaroslavi by 5p.m. Sincerely, Olga."

She wanted to sign off "with the greatest of love" but thankfully she was able to constrain herself. After all, she had told Vasily just yesterday about her family and that she loved her husband Ben Stevens. Besides, maybe her love for Vasily was similar to "shipboard romance" and when she returned to America she would get over her feelings for him. As she was thinking of all of this his name came up on her computer and he had this reply: "Dear Olga, You have made me so happy. My mother has expressed a desire to meet you also. If you can come to the Gorka restaurant you can park your car in their lot and I will take you to the hospital. After our visit we can return and have our dinner there. Can't wait to see you. Love, Vasily."

Olga called her mum at the dacha to tell her she would be meeting an old college girlfriend in Yaroslavi, and might be staying with her overnight so not to worry because she would be home long before they returned from the dacha. Olga understood that eventually she would need to reveal to her parents that Bill Bond had a son living in Yaroslavi and she had visited him. After all, they knew Bill well when he spent time with them in May of 2011. Also he sat with them in the family box when Olga married Ben. But explaining everything to them now was way too complicated.

For the remainder of the day all she could think of was her meeting with Vasily the next day. It was just yesterday that she was with him at the Romanoff Forest Ecotel and her anxiety to see him again was a real concern. To clear her mind she decided to go over to the Athletic Club to exercise and do some serious swimming. When she was living here as a young woman, it was her favorite pastime especially when she was under stress. Now, here she was, decades later trying to deal with a situation which could easily get out of control. She understood she was a married woman and to fall in love with another man this quickly would be problematic to say the least, if she acted on her strong feelings for him. Just the massage she received yesterday would invoke a strong reaction from her parents if they were to learn of her indiscretion. The fact that it was done in a private cabin by a man she just met would only make things worse. And heaven forbid, if she ever decided to tell them and that she had a very intense orgasm they would probably disown her. Of course that would be one confession she would never make, not even to her priest.

Before retiring for the evening she decided to send an e-mail to Ben and a few friends in the USA. The following morning she was well rested and in high spirits. Her first chore was to take her rented car down to have it waxed and polished. She would wear the other summer dress Inna had made for her. It was a blend of her two favorite colors (red and black) and when she put it on she looked stunning to say the least.

Now, at last, she was on her way to Yaroslavi. She knew the city well from her teen age years when she dated a hockey player on the Yaroslavi Locomotiv team that had won a Russian league championship. While driving there she began to think how bizarre things seemed. All her expenses for her trip including her car rental and dress were from a fund she inherited from Bill Bond. Now, she was on the way to meet with his son, and Galina, the woman he made love to back in 1982 during a brief two week romance.

The time had gone by quickly and now she was pulling into the parking area of the Gorka restaurant. And there was Vasily, directing her to a parking space he had reserved for her. In his charcoal suit and red tie she thought he was the most handsome man she had ever seen. And her, in her red and black low cut cotton dress, they were without a doubt the perfect couple.

They gave each other an affectionate hug as he led her to his car for the 10 minute drive to the hospital to visit his mum. When they got there she was sitting up in bed propped up by two pillows. She had her hair done and was wearing a pretty blue gown and when Vasily went over to hug her he introduced her to Olga at the same time. At 71, she was too young to die and it was apparent that she was another reason Vasily was so extremely good looking. Little did Bill or Galina realize at the time, during their brief romance, that they would have such an outstanding son in everyway. Yes there was no mistake that Bill Bond was his father because their profiles were similar but Galina, even at her age and with her ailment, was still a most beautiful lady.

Olga and Galina were now in full embrace and the tears from both were profuse when Olga broke the silence with, "I feel so privileged to have met you." Galina went on to express how proud she was of Olga for her brave and heroic action that freed Bill from house arrest in Chelyabinsk. Here were two ladies over three decades apart in age who were brought together because of their commonality to Bill Bond. About an hour into their visit a nurse came by to remind them that her doctor didn`t want any visits over 45 minutes. They understood because it was apparent she was already weak so they gave her a hug and a few more tears were shed as they left the room.

When they got back to the Gorka restaurant it was truly unique. On the first floor there was a bar, a bowling alley, and pool table while the restaurant was on the second floor. Their offerings were both traditional and international. They chose a large plate of small traditional choices that was meant to be shared. The offerings were delightful and delicious. After dinner Vasily suggested they go to the first floor for a few frames of bowling and Olga accepted enthusiastically wanting to extend the time with him as long as possible.

After bowling they went to the bar for a light drink when Vasily suggested, "It is already 10p.m and you should not drive to Kostroma this late in the evening. Please come to my house for the night and we will have an opportunity to discuss matters of mutual interest."

This was what Olga was hoping for and without hesitation she responded, "Thank you very much I accept your kind offer and while there I would be anxious to engage in a conversation concerning your desire to obtain dual USA/Russian citizenship."

She followed him to his house and was surprised to see it was a single family home with enough parking for a half dozen vehicles. She picked up her overnight bag and as they entered it was obvious that Vasily was a man of some means because Olga recognized that the furniture and art work were of excellent quality.

"Why don't you use this bedroom to get into something more comfortable and then we can go to the great room to have a conversation. There is an adjoining bathroom so make yourself at home. She had decided to wear a less suggestive night gown not wanting him to think she was trying to entice him into some situation that might be uncomfortable.

When she got to the great room he was sitting in a chair wearing his jogging attire or at the least something similar. Nevertheless, the outfit was designed to show off his perfect physique. "You look very nice Olga and please sit down on this special chair my mother owned for over 40 years. I recently had it upholstered. I call it "my chair for honored guests only" so I hope you know you are very special."

Olga reciprocated, "Yes I do feel very special because I met a very exceptional lady this evening and to sit in her chair is a very distinct honor for me."

"Now I hope you don't mind if we can spend some time discussing the matter concerning your desire to obtain a dual USA/Russian citizenship." Vasily was excited that she took the initiative, "Yes, in my first letter to you I asked if it were possible for you to help me in any way regarding this matter when I discovered my biological father was Bill Bond."

She began to tell him everything regarding their relationship starting when she first met him on the deck at Hannah's in the summer of 2010. She didn't leave anything out and when she got to where they were re-united in Chincoteague in 2022 just a few years ago she explained. "When I discovered my husband had a mistress he was unwilling to give up I was distraught. I had not seen Bill Bond in many years and when I learned he had moved from Russia to Chincoteague, just a 70 minute drive from my home in Easton, Maryland I sought him out to provide comfort and solace. As it turned out, your dad and I had several affairs over a period of time and some of his DNA (sperm) ended up on my bra. For some reason, I decided to put the bra in a plastic bag and put it in one of my storage lockers. You might be interested in knowing your father was still a very romantic guy even at his advanced age. I hope you will not be disappointed in me for what I did."

Almost immediately Vasily understood the significance of her confession and he got out of his chair and put his arms around her, "Of course I am not disappointed in you, I am very grateful. Are you saying to me you would consider providing that sample to an immigration judge?" Olga did not hesitate in her response, "Yes I would, but of course I would ask the judge to give me a private hearing if that were possible. Regardless, I would still do it no matter what rules or venue are set forth."

With that Vasily again put his arms around her and kissed her forehead. "You are truly a remarkable woman. It is past midnight and I know you must be completely exhausted. Of course I too must get up early in the morning so why don't we retire for the evening. I am sure you will find your bed comfortable since I just purchased one of the very best ones on the market."

With that they embraced tightly and although they both wanted to be in the same bed neither wanted to suggest it so they went into their separate bedrooms. Olga was very tired and ordinarily she would be asleep in moments, but knowing a man she cared so much about was in a bedroom right across the hallway she wanted to be awake just in case she heard his voice asking if he could join her. But she understood he was too much of a gentleman and there was little chance that would happen.

Since she was a married woman and already feeling guilty for what happened in Cabin #8 in the Romanoff complex she knew she could not take the initiative. So, she decided to pleasure herself while thinking of him and within minutes she was sound asleep.

When she awoke in the morning she could smell the aroma of bacon so she got up took a quick shower and went to the kitchen. "Hi Olga, I trust you got a good night of rest because you look so refreshed for this early in the morning." She decided to tell a little white lie, "Yes, thank you, I went right to sleep within minutes. You were right, your mattress was most comfortable and I will have to remember the brand when we are in need of a new one."

After having their bacon, eggs and pancakes it was now time for Olga to head back to Kostroma. They were now at the front door saying their goodbyes and each promised to keep in touch with e-mails. The drive back to Kostroma was one of deep reflection for Olga. It was a crazy thought that entered her mind already thinking of asking Ben for a divorce. It was such a stupid thought because she had already assumed that Vasily would want to marry her. There were probably a dozen women thinking the same thing.

She could never forget the intense orgasm she had in the Romanov Forest cabin during her massage. To think that whoever landed him would be getting this service once a week was enough to make any woman jealous. But, she knew she had to keep her emotions in check for fear of turning him off altogether. For now, she had the upper hand in their relationship because she had the DNA evidence that could give him the dual citizenship he so badly wanted. It was going to require a lot of time and effort to work through all the red tape but she was more than willing to go through all the hoops if necessary, to maintain her advantage. But now, she had to shift her thoughts to her kids and parents because they would be back from the dacha in the morning.

When she arrived at her parents' home, she called her mum at the dacha and told her she had stayed with her girlfriend in Yaroslavi, and they had great fun reminiscing about the good old times, changing boyfriends on a whim as if they were nothing more than a commodity. They had a great time at the Gorky Pub having dinner and bowling a few frames. Of course this was all a made up story for now. Later, when it was the right time she would tell her parents it was Vasily Sokolov that she was with.

When she finished talking to her mum she checked her e-mails and received one each from the men in her life. First she would read the one from Ben: "Hi Honey, just wanted you to know that I really miss you and love you very much. I can't believe I will have to wait 45 more days before I hold you in my arms. I took care of all the chores you instructed me to do. Some of the girls' friends have been knocking on the door asking when Marina and Anastasia were coming back and they were very disappointed when I told them it would be the end of July. Got to leave for work now but will be thinking of you every day. You are everything to me, Ben."

After receiving such a wonderful letter, how could she be thinking of another man? She felt so guilty but yet she was helpless to deal with the situation in a responsible way. After all, she was not a teenager anymore when having multiple boyfriends was common place. She was a married 40 year old woman and she and Ben had exchanged vows at the Ipatiev Monastery right here in Kostroma just 12 years ago. How could she ever forget that day and the following one when he delivered the keystone speech during that time of celebration and cooperation between Russia and the USA.

Now she would read the e-mail from Vasily: "My Dear Olga, I can't express to you in adequate words how much our day yesterday meant to me. To see how you and my mother bonded brought tears to my eyes. In a few weeks I will no longer have her in my life. I know I will be lonely because she means everything to me. And then, to think in 45 short days you will no longer be here in Russia. It is really too sad for me to contemplate. Also, I must confess, it took every ounce of my will power to keep from coming to your door last night to ask if you would consider coming to my bedroom. I hope you will not think less of me for this admission. Love you, Vasily."

So, what was she to do? For many women, having two outstanding men vying for her affection would be nirvana. And after all, even today, in some parts of Russia having a wife and mistress was considered a status symbol. Her own husband, Ben Stevens had a mistress for a period of time, no doubt showering her with gifts while getting sexual favors in return. So, maybe for her, that would be the card to play at least for now.

She eventually told her parents about Vasily being the son of Bill Bond and needless to say they were in total disbelief. Of course, she did not reveal to them that she had an intimate relationship with him over the period of time she was in Russia.

Olga Returns to America

As the weeks passed her and Vasily found other opportunities to be together. The love and respect they had for each other grew stronger by the day, but in reality, any shared future together seemed like a hopeless dream. The morning Olga feared and dreaded had finally arrived. She would be going back home to Easton, Md. USA and just the thought of never seeing Vasily again put her in a state loneliness and depression, as she packed her dad`s van for the trip to the Domodedovo Airport in Moscow. Her daughters, Marina and Anastasia were anxious to join their friends in Easton but they would miss Russia and their grandparents.

On the flight back home Olga`s mind shifted back and forth between Ben and Vasily and how she would mentally deal with a situation that had no apparent viable solution. Before landing at Dulles in Washington she checked her e-mails one last time and Vasily gave her the sad news that his mother Galina passed away during the night in her sleep. She wanted to get right back on a return flight to Russia to be with Vasily but understood it was not a practical thing to do. She sent a quick response expressing her sorrow, and how impressed she was with his mother`s spirit, although she only knew her for that one short hour while at the hospital in Yaroslavi. Olga and Galina had a common bond that could never be severed because of their relationship with Bill Bond.

When they arrived at the airport, Ben was waiting in the receiving line to greet them, as Marina and Anastasia ran toward their dad, where they exchanged hugs and many words of how much they missed each other. When they arrived home in Easton the first thing was to re-connect with all their friends in the immediate neighborhood. For their first few nights in bed together Ben could not have been more passionate using love techniques similar to Vasily's, but their method of delivery was so much different. It seemed as if their marriage had worked through all the difficulties she endured during Ben's infidelity. However, her time with Vasily had made an indelible impression, and dealing with the emotions she felt for him, would be a challenge in the months ahead.

During the first week of Olga's return Ben would shower her with flowers and candy and other gifts including underwear from Victoria's Secret. He would bring body oil and whipped cream into the bedroom for fun and pleasure using his tongue in ways she had not received in the past. It was a change she welcomed enthusiastically and she made every effort to reciprocate to be certain she delivered pleasures to him of equal gratification.

After a fortnight at home she knew she would need to set the wheels into motion in efforts to obtain dual citizenship for Vasily. She would need to accomplish this in a sort of surreptitious way making sure Ben was not aware of her involvement at least for now. It was a reminder of her days in the RIS. She would use the internet and Google to search out the methodology necessary to begin the process.

She had brought back two specimens of Vasily's DNA, and now she had possession of both his and Bill Bond's sperm. If Ben knew of this what would he think? She called an immigration site first, and they instructed her to take the specimens to one of their approved laboratories to establish the credibility of the specimens, as well as any possible relationship between the two donors. This first step alone would take at least a month at a cost of five hundred dollars.

Since this was Bill Bond's sperm and that of his son she would take the money from the fund he had bequeathed to her knowing Vasily would re-pay her later. She would use the laboratory closest to her in Washington, D.C. This way, she could deliver them in person instead of worrying whether they would get lost in the mail. So, in the ensuing days she made an appointment for 10am on the 15th of September.

The girls were in school now, and Ben would be attending a special meeting at Langley that day, and would not be getting home until late that evening. So, she took out of storage her bra containing Bill Bond's semen, as well as the specimens she had brought back from Russia of Vasily's DNA. She packed them into containers they specified and headed for Washington. When arriving at the laboratory, a technician by the name of Molly, accepted the specimens and check, and informed Olga it would take about a month to process at which time she would be notified by e-mail of the results.

Waiting was like a mother in her eighth month of pregnancy. During that period she would go out to lunch and do little short shopping excursions with her two best friends wanting everything to look as normal as possible. Then, on October the 13th she received this e-mail from the laboratory: "The results proved conclusively that the two specimens you submitted showed a very close relationship similar to a father and son. There is no chance that the two could not be closely related in the manner in which we stated. Please pick up your test results and specimens as soon as possible."

Olga was elated to a point where she felt compelled to sit down and send an e-mail to Vasily: "Dear Vasily, I have been informed minutes ago that you have made it through the first hurdle. The laboratory results confirmed that Bill Bond is your biological father. I will now request from immigration authorities a meeting with one of their judges who will make the final determination regarding your request for dual citizenship. After that, the immigration board will check with their counterparts in Russia, to be sure there are no legal or criminal issues yet unresolved in your background. I can't tell you how happy I am for you because I am confident that you will be successful although it will require patience before it will finally get through all the red tape. You are always on my mind. Love, Olga"

Within hours Olga got this response: "My Dear Olga, I don't know how to thank you for all that you are doing for me. Please let me know what your total expenses are and I will send you a credit card you can access for cash. Since my separation from my wife five years ago, I had been very lonely until I met you. Yes, I had ample opportunities to be with some very nice ladies but my desire was not there. I hope the day we can be together will not be too long, because since I lost my mother my desire to be with you has only intensified. Miss you and love you very much. Vasily"

Over three months had passed since she departed Russia and her desire and feelings for Vasily was stronger than ever. In fact, there were times when she was making love with Ben she was thinking only of Vasily. She understood it was a dangerous game she was playing but she was helpless to change the direction of the emotional roller coaster she was on.

The following week she began calling immigration offices, and after a while, she was able to connect with a very nice and highly capable woman who seemed more than willing to assist her, in arranging an appointment with an immigration judge. After the nice lady consulted with a colleague she set a date of Nov. 16th at 1p.m at their building at 6th and H Street N.W. Things were moving even quicker than she anticipated, and what was even more encouraging, she would not be required to bring the actual DNA samples, just the laboratory results.

However, Olga would be required to answer many questions regarding the donors and any history she may have had with them. Up to now, she was able to conceal everything from her husband and was hoping the judge would not ask her how she was able to obtain the donors DNA samples. Since the meeting would be in D.C. she arranged with a girlfriend living in Silver Spring to spend the night with her. After her meeting that day they would attend a Caps/Penguin hockey match-up at 7:30 that evening. Ben would be taking several days off to be with their daughters during her two day visit. She knew she would be nervous when the day of her meeting arrived so she called her doctor to get some medicine that would calm her nerves.

And now the day arrived and she got off to a 9a.m start wanting time to have a light lunch in Silver Spring before parking her car at her girlfriend's house. She took the metro downtown to within two blocks of the immigration offices. Walking down the corridors with her brief case that contained the DNA results seemed so unreal. Over a 15 year period she and Bill Bond had shared so much and little did she realize, that just 15 months after his passing, she would be involved with his 43 year old son. When she got to the door where she was instructed to report, a lady led her to a small room with a desk and two chairs and said that Judge Jimmy Walker would be with her shortly.

Within minutes he arrived and introduced himself, "Good afternoon, my name is Jimmy Walker and I will be handling your case, introduce yourself and briefly describe your reasons for being here."

"My name is Olga Kornakova and I am here to represent a friend of mine by the name of Vasily Sokolov, a Russian citizen, who is trying to obtain dual Russia/USA citizenship. In my briefcase, I have DNA results from an approved laboratory, that shows conclusively that an American citizen by the name of Bill Bond, now deceased, is his biological father."

The judge then removed his glasses from its case and asked to see the results from the lab. As he studied the report Olga was making an assessment of him. She thought him to be about 50 and no doubt a sportsman. His graying well groomed hair, tanned face, and piercing green eyes gave the appearance of someone that the ladies would love to share some time with. His face exuded both confidence and kindness and it was easy to observe that he took care of his body with regular workouts.

"Well, Ms. Kornakova from what I have discerned from these results your client most certainly has the right to dual-citizenship providing there are no criminal or legal issues pending, or not yet resolved in his native Russia. Of course the immigration board will make that determination when they contact their counter-parts in Russia. Now, instead of asking you a lot of questions which I am under obligation to do maybe it would be best to explain how you got to know Mr. Sokolov, and why he chose you to represent him, since most times this is a job for a lawyer."

Olga began to explain how she had met Bill Bond at Hannah's in the summer of 2010 their near-death experience at Chincoteague that year and their continuing friendship until his death in the spring of 2025. The following year, she received a letter from Vasily Sokolov, where he explained that his mother, Galina, revealed to him of having a brief romance with Bill Bond during her visit to America in 1982 while visiting her sister. When Galina returned to Russia, and learned she was pregnant, she decided not to tell Bill Bond she was carrying his baby. About a year after Vasily's birth, Galina met a man by the name of Vitali Sokolov and eventually they married. For almost 43 years Vasily assumed Vitali was his biological father. By the way, Vitali passed away several years ago."

"Well, Ms. Kornakova, that was a nice synopsis, leaving much for my imagination and interpretation. I don't need every detail that could possibly be embarrassing, although I can see no good reason for it, because obviously, there is a lot of caring love in your story, which sometimes, gets manifested in different ways. When it does, we must never be ashamed. You have provided all the information I will need to make my determination and you can be confident I will rule in a favorable way to your client's request. You have represented him well. You can be sure that what you have revealed today will be held in strict confidence. After my ruling, the documents will be sealed and can only be accessed to settle a criminal case which is highly unlikely. Now, I will have time to get in a round of golf and you are welcome to join me if you are so inclined."

Of course Olga recognized his offer was just a gesture of kindness and stated to him she didn't know the difference between a tennis ball and a golf ball. They shook hands, and as she walked out of the room and headed for the metro she was especially grateful that she met an exceptional human being, not some stick to the rules bureaucrat, looking for a titillating tale of sex and heaven knows what else?

There was little doubt in her mind he understood that she was romantically involved with both Bill Bond and Vasily but being the gentleman he was, he shielded her from the embarrassing questions he had every right to ask. When she got on the metro she was in a state of exultation. At the Caps/Penguin match-up that evening with her friend she not only watched a classic game which the Caps won two to one, and her hero, Alex Ovechkin, got an assist and scored the winning goal.

Driving home the next day to Easton she thought how lucky she was to have gotten Judge Jimmy Walker to hear her case. He was a real gentleman and his kindness and understanding would always be a pleasant memory. Now, she could always feel comfortable in the future if she had to go before a tribunal for any reason.

When she walked in the house Ben and the girls were playing chess and she immediately went over to give all three a big hug. It had been a while since Ben had seen her in such high spirits. "Wow Olga, maybe you should go watch the Caps more often." She was feeling guilty because even though she was happy for the Caps, and her hero Alex Ovechkin, her great happiness was brought about by what she was able to accomplish for Vasily Sokolov.

A Special Night for Ben

There was no question that she was in a very amorous mood and she decided she wanted to reward Ben because not only was he a real sport taking the time to be with the girls for two days but the encouragement and support he had given her while she was in Russia for two months. She warned him in advance she wanted to do some exciting things in the bedroom that evening. He again made reference to her being in Washington to watch the Caps. "I am going to see you get to a few more Cap games this year if I am going to be the recipient of all this special attention."

For the rest of the day she began to slip into the bedroom various items she would need to implement her plan; body oil, extra sheets, plastic bands for tie down purposes, phantom of the opera mask, garter belts, her music cassette player and her favorite lingerie. While Ben and the girls were watching their favorite family television show she begged off claiming to be tired since returning from her trip. She spread a double layer of sheets on their soft carpet bedroom floor similar to the way Vasily Sokolov had done at the Ecotel cabin in Russia a few months earlier.

After the girls went to bed in their isolated bedroom upstairs, Olga slipped on her mask, garters, and sexy red and black underwear. When Ben completed his shower she began to play her phantom of the opera music while drying him off, using both her towel while blowing her breath on his most sensual areas. After which she led him to the makeshift bed on the floor where she would begin the massage she had carefully planned. She tied his arms and legs to the bed posts and chairs nearby and began to pour body oil on his navel and groin, massaging those areas with circular movements similar to the motion

Vasily had administered to her in Russia. Unable to move his arms and legs he requested she move her vulva close to his lips and she did so. It was a most satisfying experience for both with Olga achieving a most gratifying orgasm. Both used their tongues and lips in the most sensuous way to achieve ultimate satisfaction.

Over their 12 year marriage Olga had never been this bold and wondered if she had been more experimental maybe Ben would not have felt the need for a mistress. On the other hand, maybe it would have just whetted his appetite wanting to have similar experiences with different women. She then released him from his bondage and he gave her an appreciative hug as she gathered up the sheets. As they lay side by side in bed huddled together it would be an evening that neither would soon forget.

The next morning as Ben was leaving for work they embraced as if they were newlyweds. The four day Thanksgiving holiday was just a week away and Olga was looking forward to not only their time on the beach, at Cancun, but a renewed and vibrant relationship with Ben. This vacation had been planned to celebrate her 40th birthday. It would be a belated celebration since Ben had attended a two day seminar in Norfolk on Nov. 1, which was her actual birthday. Although things were going well at home her mind was still on Vasily and wanting to assure him that things were on track she wrote a him a short letter.

"Dear Vasily, My meeting with the immigration judge went well. He almost assured me that your application for dual citizenship would be approved. The only hurdle remaining is the immigration board that will check out your past with their counterparts in Russia to be sure there are no unresolved issues relating to legal matters. How long that will take I can't predict, but I am confident by the spring of next year your application will be granted. Love, Olga." A few hours later Vasily responded again expressing his thanks and love.

The more Olga thought about Vasily the more concerned she became about their relationship. It could possibly jeopardize his position if Russian officials discovered he was having an affair with the wife of a high ranking CIA officer. It was also possible that immigration officials here in the USA would not look kindly on his application if they became aware of the situation. As the week passed she understood it was something she would have to deal with in a responsible way.

Up to now, if Ben found out about her infidelity she could always claim it was a lingering desire to get even for his past indiscretions. But now, their marriage was healing well, and as the four of them boarded the Air Mexico flight out of BWI for Cancun everyone was in high spirits. Ben understood that Olga having her 40th birthday was reason to celebrate in style. He had chosen to stay at the Marriott Resort and Spa reserving two rooms on different floors. Their daughters, Marina and Anastasia, now eleven and eight, felt they were old enough to be treated as young adults.

The Marriott had all the amenities you would expect from a five star resort including sandy white beaches, fitness center, water sports, exercise classes, restaurants, several outdoor swimming pools, massage therapy, laundry services and so much more. It was a place that would put anyone into a romantic mood and she was looking forward to having more bedroom games with Ben. When they arrived, Olga couldn't wait to take advantage of some of their amenities, and she immediately signed up for the exercise classes and massage therapy. It would not be the kind of massage administered by Vasily when she visited Russia. No internal touching this time. When Olga was not with Ben, you could almost always find him either at the exercise facility or at the beach taking in the rays or doing his four mile walk or trot; two miles up and two miles back. On Thanksgiving Day management set up a buffet that was fit for a King and his Queen.

Like all short vacations they end way too soon. It was now time to fly back to Baltimore and then drive to Easton. Marina and Anastasia had met some friends their age and became pretty proficient in the art of scuba diving. Soon, they would return to school and Ben would be back on the job. While in Cancun, Olga hadn't thought much about Vasily but she understood it was time to make a crucial decision regarding any future liaisons with him. So, after much soul searching, she sat down and wrote this letter.

"My Dear Vasily, I have spent many hours in thought on how I should write this letter. There is so much I want to say. Because I was so selfish, and my desire to spend quality time with you, I could not see past the end of my nose. I am the wife of a high ranking CIA official and if the media or others learned that our friendship extended into the bedroom, your name would be tarnished and your career possibly ruined. I won't allow that to happen. I have been working on my marriage and things are better than they have been in a long time. Since Ben has given up his mistress he has given me so much love and attention. I owe it to him, and my daughters, to give it my best effort to be a good wife and mother."

I know one day you will get your dual citizenship and you will be able to travel to the states and perhaps we can have dinner but we must not allow ourselves to have a physical relationship. (Not even one of those unforgettable massages.) For the sake of your career and our families we must make that sacrifice. You are a good man and Bill Bond would be very proud of you. Your mum Galina, thought you were special and she was so right. I must sign off for now because I hear my daughters coming in from school. Good luck in all your future endeavors. I know you will continue to be successful no matter what challenge you undertake. Love, Olga."

It was the most difficult letter she had ever written but she knew it was the only responsible thing to do. When she first met him, she was so smitten by his good looks and gentle demeanor her desire to be with him in a private and physical way, overwhelmed her good judgment at the time. It was she who set the wheels in motion that led to the cottage at the Romanov Forest in Russia. And now, it was her responsibility to take the initiative to put some brakes on this runaway train before too many lives were shattered. Within a short time, she heard back from Vasily, and it was about what she expected since he was such an understanding and pragmatic person.

"My Dear Olga, How can I express my gratitude for all you have accomplished? Yes, I knew you were married from the start and you will never know the guilt and shame I felt at the time. With my divorce now finalized, and my mother near death, I was badly in need of a woman's love, so, when you came into my life it was as if some divine force had granted it. Thank God for your strength and fortitude for undertaking the task of bringing me back to reality. I am so happy that I can look forward to having dinner with you in the future and my hope is that our friendship will continue in a more realistic and sustainable way. Gratefully yours, Vasily."

Vasily begins a New Business

It would be their last two letters until Vasily sent her a brief note to express his appreciation when he learned he had received all his papers confirming he had achieved full USA citizenship. He had travelled to New York several times during the summer and fall of 2027 to discuss a business proposition with the Morgan Stanley brokerage firm but he and Olga could not schedule any dinner engagements because of time constraints.

Vasily wanted to go into the cement and concrete business in Russia and he purchased sizable acreage between Yaroslavi and Kostroma for this endeavor. There was a similar type government facility at the same location during the Soviet days but after 1991 when a market based economy emerged the site was abandoned. He was able to purchase the site at a bargain price and he was in New York to inquire about a possible loan for construction of the facility and infrastructure improvements as well as the purchase of concrete hauling trucks.

The acreage was rich in the three main raw materials for production of cement and concrete; rock, stone, water and sand. There was also a chemical company nearby where they could acquire the silica alumina and limestone that would be required for the process he intended to utilize. Even better, the old Soviet company had left huge piles of sand and gravel and this would save a lot of money in mining costs during the initial period when operating funds would be crucial.

Vasily understood from his position as Administrator of Roads and Bridges in Yaroslavi there were thousands of projects in the pipeline for infrastructure improvements. The necessity to repair and construct roads, sidewalks, and bridges were acute, and he would attempt to convince government officials the need to cycle some funds from oil and natural gas revenue to finance these necessary projects. Morgan Stanley was trying to establish a presence in this part of Russia so they sent their Vice President of Sales, Ron Brown, to Yaroslavi to meet with Vasily, to assess the site and prospects for its success. He spent an entire week there as Vasily's house guest, inspecting the site and he was not only impressed about its possibility but was excited to get things underway as quickly as possible.

To expedite things, Mr. Brown and Vasily went to the internet to study other designs of similar facilities in other parts of the world and bingo they found one in West Australia that would work here. For just ten thousand rubles they could purchase the design and specifications. This was a huge find because now they could begin the bidding process as soon as their financing was established.

It was now an easy job to put all the figures together knowing what their costs would be for the facility and the concrete hauling trucks he would need. Vasily decided he could serve as the general contractor saving time and money. To cover all the costs and allowing a slight fudge factor, Vasily would need a 22 million dollar loan. Ron Brown would go to New York to arrange the loan and Vasily would go to Moscow to see what support he could obtain from the Russian government.

Because of his position he was able to obtain a quick appointment with the board of Planning and Development, a government entity set up in 1991 to assist enterprising entrepreneurs to start new businesses. Their dual role was to encourage foreign and private investors to participate in their new market based economy. When Vasily informs them that Morgan Stanley is seriously considering awarding him a 22 million dollar loan the 12 member board looked at each other in disbelief. If this were true, they were more than ready to assist him.

The Russian government had big plans for the Moscow to Kostroma corridor which included a modern six lane highway, a new state of the art airport, and a connecting bridge across the Volga along with modern office buildings and housing for the up and coming middle class. There was an actual shortage of concrete and cement contractors in the region so they made this proposal; Vasily would get a good percentage of the contracts for the work at the market price for cement and concrete, but in return, he would have to resign his post as Administrator of Roads and Bridges in Yaroslavi immediately.

He loved his job, but he was more than willing to make the sacrifice, because now he would have his own company and this gave him a feeling of independence and accomplishment that transcended all other considerations. There were ample funds to maintain a payroll for the first six months after he obtained his initial contracts. Besides, he had made good investments on Wall Street over the years so to maintain an adequate style of living over that period of time would not be a problem.

The following week he received a call from Ron Brown that his loan was approved by a unanimous vote of the board and the funds would be placed in the banks of his choice immediately. Needless to say, he was ecstatic. He could now begin to line up contractors and sub-contractors. His first call was to the Oshkosh Corporation in Wisconsin, USA to order his concrete hauling trucks. The dirt road leading to his site would be his second home so he ordered a heavy Ram pickup truck to make those trips.

The ensuing years were among the happiest of his life. His company was a huge success with enough profits to pay back his loan early. He was wealthy beyond his most optimistic expectations but there was something missing in his life. He had no wife and children, and although he was still in the prime of his life his happiness was not complete. Yes, he had a wonderful 10 year marriage to Magdalina but her career was more important than children and that eventually lead to their separation and divorce. And how could he ever forget Olga Kornakova and the way she helped him gain his USA citizenship that opened so many doors for him.

The Search

Now he had this burning desire to learn more about his biological father Bill Bond and those he associated with in his life other than his mother Galina. He loved Russia and would never consider living anywhere else on a permanent basis. In fact, he was still living in his modest but comfortable home in Yaroslavia. He felt a strong bond to the USA because that is where he secured the loan that got his business up and running. The word bond had a significant meaning to him since this was his father's surname. So he decided since his mother never gave him a middle name he would now be Vasily Bond Sokolov.

Olga had made him aware of his father's long time spouse Betsy Bond, now deceased, but there were rumors he had been involved with a number of Russian women after their separation. He had this inner compulsion to locate them and learn more about this most interesting man whose DNA was flowing through his veins. He wanted to write to Olga to see if she could fill in some of the blanks, but he was afraid that she might interpret his letter as an attempt to re-kindle the flame that existed between them some years ago, so he decided against it.

His mum, Galina, had told him that during the Spy Exchange Program he had received a lot of notoriety and thought she had heard he had lived for some time in St. Petersburg. Olga, also mentioned this. So, there is where he would start. His ex-wife, Magdalina Brezhneva was living there and had a very successful gynecology practice so maybe he would call her in advance and invite her out to dinner one evening while there.

When he called Magdalina insisted that he stay at her four bedroom townhouse for however long he would be in St. Petersburg. And he reasoned why not, since after their separation they would correspond, and there was never any ill-will between them. He took the Sapsan bullet train from Moscow and had arranged in advance for a car rental on a day to day basis not knowing how long he would be there.

When he arrived in St. Petersburg it was about 6p.m and his rental car was waiting so he drove over to Magdalina's townhouse. She had always maintained her last name of Brezhneva as most professionals do, when establishing their credentials in medical school, or whatever career path one would take. She met him at the door and they hugged because both had great respect for each other and their respective accomplishments.

Magdalina had prepared a traditional Russian dinner and their conversation moved to the intervening years after their separation. When Vasily told her his reason for visiting St. Petersburg was to learn more about his biological father Bill Bond she was stunned, because she had not heard of this; thinking his birth father was Vitali Sokolov. "My goodness Vasily, you took me by complete surprise. Also, the name Bill Bond rings a bell. I heard that name mentioned by someone just a few weeks ago." Vasily said it was probably just a lingering thing in her mind since Bill Bond had received a lot of notoriety during the Spy Exchange Program.

"I was a student at the time, trying to pass my engineering exams, and never paid much attention to the event, but now in retrospect, after learning he was my father, I think I do remember his name from that period."

"No, no Vasily, one of my recent patients mentioned his name to me. Her husband, a taxi driver, would bring her to appointments and apparently he knew Bill Bond very well." Vasily was excited because if true, it would be the time and place to start his investigation. Magdalina really got into the spirit of the moment and maybe this would be an opportunity to use her long constrained passion to be an amateur sleuth.

Her favorite books were detective novels and she wanted to assist Vasily. "I keep duplicate copies of my files here at my home office so let me go there to see if I can find her name."

About 15 minutes later she rejoined Vasily as he was finishing up his bread pudding. "Her name is Isodora Fiske. I will call her in the morning. She is due for one more visit to be sure there was no re-occurrence of the condition of which she was being treated." Vasily became emotional that his ex-wife was anxious to assist him offering to use his skills as a masseur later that evening. She accepted without delay, remembering her weekly massage routine when they were together as a married couple.

As she undressed later that evening it almost felt like the first night of their honeymoon so many years ago. Vasily would give her a more traditional massage rather than the more intimate one he had provided to Olga that memorable day in the cabin at the Romanov Forest. Nevertheless, when he had finished his service for her they showered together and extended their pleasure with reciprocal oral love.

They both got up early the next morning with a light breakfast of oatmeal and toast. Magdalina had a busy day ahead but foremost in her mind was to call Isidora Fiske to see if she could come in early at her downtown office. After reaching her she explained to Isidora that she would have to go out of town for a few days next week when her appointment was scheduled, and wondered if she could make it in this morning for an early 8:30 a.m check-up.

Isidora agreed it would work out fine wanting to clear her mind regarding her condition as soon as possible. Her husband would always wait for her in his taxi at the office parking lot and Vasily would also be there to introduce himself telling him that Dr. Brezhneva was an associate and he had a 9:15 appointment. When Vasily went over to the taxi to introduce himself to the driver he expressed a desire to hire him for a 4 hour tour of the city at whatever day was convenient for him.

"My name is Arno and after I take my wife home, today would work for me."

Vasily agreed it would also work for him and Arno said he would come back to the parking lot to pick him up. After Arno and his wife left Vasily went into Magdalina's office to tell her of his plans and when they met later this evening they would go out to dinner. When

Arno returned and Vasily got into his taxi he decided to get right to the point; "Arno, my name is Vasily Bond Sokolov and my biological father was a man by the name of Bill Bond, is there any chance you knew him?"

Arno seemed to recognize this was some kind of a setup but he didn't hesitate one minute to answer, "Yes, I knew him very well and he left me a tidy sum of money when he passed away in 2025. I can see he was your father because your profiles and face structure is very similar. Your papa was a good and generous man and you should be very proud of him." At this time they shook hands as if they were brothers who had not seen each other since childhood. "Can you take me to the part of the city where my father lived?"

"Yes, not only where he resided but to the cemetery where Vera Petrova's remains are deterred." Vasily was puzzled because he had never heard of this woman.

"What connection did she have to him?" Arno gave him a sheepish look not realizing he was unaware of Vera Petrova's importance in his father's life.

"She was the reason he came to St. Petersburg in the first place. They were to be married, but a day before his arrival her van was struck head on by a beer delivery truck and she succumbed a few days later."

This took Vasily by complete surprise knowing his father was in the autumn of his years at the time. "How old was Vera at the time?" Arno guessed her to be about 40 "but age was not even a consideration to either of them because they were of kindred spirit." When they arrived at the apartment building where Bill Bond rented his first floor flat Arno pointed to it saying, "I was with him the day he put down his retainer and since he only had two pieces of luggage he moved in the same day. He actually renewed his two year lease several times living there a total of seven years."

They drove to the Blue Bridge where Vera Petrova's life essentially ended. She lived in a comatose state for several days before her life support system was unplugged. After that, Arno and Vasily visited the cemetery where Vera's remains were interred.

"There is one more place I want you to see before the day ends. For some reason, your papa had a great fascination for it." When they arrived there, Arno explained it was the house and property where the RIS Deputy Commander was living at the time. "Mr. Bond would ask me to drive by there on occasion, and his eyes were fixated on a specific wing of the house." Vasily was intrigued by this bit of information and asked Arno if he remembered the name of the Deputy Commander at the time.

"Yes, but I will only tell you, because you are the son of the man I respected so much. Her name was Dasha Brumel, and they were seen around town at various venues together and there was some speculation, they had an intimate relationship for a short period of time. As I remember, it was about two years after Vera Petrova's passing when Ms. Brumel came to St. Petersburg to assume her duties."

Vasily had never met Ms. Brumel, but he knew she was a high ranking official in the government and seeing her picture many times in various publications, he remembered she was a very attractive woman. As their day was ending and Arno took him to his car they again shook hands with Vasily handing him an envelope, "There is a little extra in there, I hope you will use some of it it to purchase a nice gift for your wife."

As he drove back to Magdalina's townhouse he understood that it would take a while to digest and interpret all he had seen and heard today. When he arrived she was waiting, "Don't tell me anything yet about your day today. We can talk about everything while having dinner. I have made reservations at the Taleon and if you haven't eaten there you will be in for a very pleasant surprise. Now get yourself ready and put on this sport coat I bought for you today."

He agreed that dinner at the Taleon was a great idea because although he had never eaten there its reputation was wide spread. "But only if I can compensate you for the sport coat and you understand the dinner is my treat." In a kidding way she looked at him, "Just go ahead and get ready and quit trying to show me how well off you are." On the way over he could not contain his anxiety, "Are you familiar with the name Dasha Brumel?" She looked at him quizzically, "Of course, it is like asking me if I ever heard of Putin or Medvedev. Why do you ask?"

Vasily paused for a moment, "She was once the Deputy Commander of the RIS here in St. Petersburg and there was a rumor at the time that her and my father had a brief intimate relationship according to Arno." Magdalina was very familiar with the history of political figures both past and present. "My goodness, I hope that Arno has not told too many people of this. She is no longer with the RIS having resigned to take a prestigious position at the World Bank."

Vasily assured her that he was confident that Arno had told no one else but him but of course now Magdalina knew. Although many years had passed since she was here it would still be a juicy story for the new weekly gossip publications now springing up all over Russia. But, if neither were married at the time it would not be a big deal. Except that Bill Bond was decades older than her and it would be a very interesting story even now.

When they arrived at the Taleon it was obvious by its sheer opulence and prices it was designed only for St. Petersburg's most affluent and wealthy class. After looking over their extensive menu they jointly decided to have the oven baked partridge and rack of lamb in rosemary sauce which they would share. For dessert, they decided to try their new molten lava cake that had actually been perfected in a fast food outlet in the USA. The chef's here managed to slip a little vodka and juniper into the batter which would distinguish it from its fast food originators.

Vasily's time with Magdalina was something very special. Their ten year marriage and eventual separation ended in a very amicable way, each wanting to pursue careers, which took them in different directions. After their enjoyable evening together, Vasily got up early the next morning and drove over to the neighborhood where he visited the day before with Arno and where his father had lived for over seven years. He visited some of the places where he thought his father might have frequented, and found a few older shop owners, who remembered him well and affectionately called him BB. They told Vasily his father was a kind and generous man with an irrepressible personality.

His week in St. Petersburg had passed quickly and before leaving he called Arno to thank him for his time and help in his effort to learn more about his father. Arno wanted to pass on a little more about Vera Petrova that he had forgotten to mention the day they spent together.

"She had a son by the name of Sergey Petrov who Bill Bond never met. He was now employed by Gazprom, the Russian oil and natural gas conglomerate."

After their conversation, Vasily got in his rental car and went by Magdalina's downtown office to say goodbye and vowed to find time in the future to spend some quality time together.

It was now time to go back to Moscow on Sapsan, and when he arrived at the depot the trip back was quick and exhilarating. Not only for the smooth ride, but all that he accomplished in St. Petersburg. Upon arrival, he got a taxi to his Moscow office, checked in to say hello to his employees, then, got in his van and drove to his home in Yaroslavi. After driving over to his facility that now employed over 200 people his mind could think of little else than the time he spent in St. Petersburg.

Later, at home that evening, he immediately went to the internet to his favorite search engine and typed out, "World Bank Officials" and there she was having both her e-mail and phone number listed. His curiosity was too difficult to contain so he sat down and wrote this e-mail hoping that she might, by chance, as a little more personal than her "run of the mill" variety.

"Dear Ms. Brumel, You don't know me but my name is Vasily Sokolov and I am the CEO and owner of the Sokolov Cement and Concrete Corporation in the Yaroslavi Oblast. About 6 years ago I learned that a USA citizen by the name of Bill Bond was my biological father. For this past week, I have been visiting St. Petersburg where he had lived for about seven years. During his time there you were the Deputy Commander of the Russian Intelligence Service and I thought by chance, your paths may have crossed. Since he passed away before I learned he was my father, I am trying to learn as much as possible about his life while he was living in Russia. If you could help me in this matter I would be most appreciative, Sincerely, Vasily Sokolov."

He was careful not to mention Arno, or anyone else, although he knew, that she would know, that someone had made the connection between her and his father. So now, it would be a waiting game. He knew her time and schedule would not allow her to respond to every e-mail that was sent to her. Like him, she would have her secretary screen all incoming mail bringing her attention only to those that were important or had some chance of needing her personal attention. Before retiring for the evening he sent Magdalina a note thanking her again for her hospitality and assistance while visiting St. Petersburg.

The following day he began to reflect on his future. Now approaching 50, he was able in just six years to start and build a corporation that was enormously successful bringing him great wealth. But what he was proudest of was that his company had created over 200 good jobs, with a good percentage of the profits going into a fund that paid out healthy bonuses. He thought back to Olga Kornakova who helped him gain dual citizenship and to Ron Brown who worked so diligently to help him get his initial loan from Morgan Stanley.

He was beginning to think maybe it was time to set up an employee owned corporation where he would retain 2% ownership. This would provide him with a sentimental stake in the company while providing some funds to use for charitable purposes. He would think it over for several weeks before deciding, wanting to be sure it was the thing he wanted to do.

Meanwhile, to his great surprise, he received an e-mail from Dasha Brumel in response to the one he sent to her earlier; "Dear Mr. Sokolov: I was not only surprised but actually shocked when I read your letter. Yes, I knew your father well. He had contacted me just prior to assuming my new post in St. Petersburg. We had met some years earlier when my agency was conducting an investigation of which I won't get into at this time. I had an entire month off before assuming my new duties and your father and I shared some quality time visiting historical sites and museums. On several occasions he was my guest in my new home provided to me by the government."

"At the time there was no one in my life romantically and your father had lost his potential mate Vera Petrova in a horrible accident 15 months earlier. During his several visits we shared some intimate hours. I am not ashamed to tell you this because despite our age difference our feelings for each other were real. I am most interested in how you learned Bill was your father. Maybe one day we can arrange a meeting to discuss our mutual interests. Thanks for writing to me. Dasha Brumel."

"P.S. Also, you may be interested in knowing that your father spent 14 months under house arrest in Chelyabinsk although he was an innocent man. You may wish to contact a woman by the name of Polina Botkina who was his overseer at the time. She is working out of the Moscow office of the RIS. If you like I could alert her that you may be getting in touch."

Dasha Brumel's letter provided the impetuous required to get the legal work underway to transfer his business to his employees. He decided to call Ron Brown at Morgan Stanley to discuss the matter and Ron was more than happy to arrange the transaction. Of course there would be a nice fee included for both him and his company which would be taken out of existing funds. There would be no loan or funds needed from Morgan Stanley. There was a healthy balance still remaining in corporation accounts to not only pay the fees but leave ample funds for operating expenses.

Vasily didn't want any debt for the new owners. It was quite a contrast from the time he got the corporation started having to borrow 22 million dollars from Morgan Stanley. With that loan being paid off last year the new company would not be burdened with heavy loan payments. Of course with healthy operating profits, Vasily never had a problem paying off the loan with revenues now exceeding the equivalent of 200 million dollars annually.

With Ron Brown now taking full responsibility for the transfer he could now concentrate on searching for a CEO and trying to find and talk to as many people possible who knew his father. This would be his new passion. Dasha Brumel had mentioned that a woman by the name of Polina Botkina was living and working in Moscow and he would try to contact her first. Getting in touch with a RIS employee would be a bit of a challenge since there was always someone watching who their contacts were. Since he had worked as Road and Bridges Administrator some years earlier perhaps he wouldn't be scrutinized as closely as others.

Ms. Brumel had mentioned in her letter to him that she would alert Ms. Botkina that he would be getting in touch. He wrote a short e-mail to Ms. Brumel that he would gladly accept her offer. In fact, she was actually kind enough to arrange a time and place convenient to both. Their meeting would take place at the Radisson Hotel Restaurant in the Arabat section of Moscow on the 10th of this month at 6p.m.

When the evening arrived a most attractive lady greeted Vasily as he walked into the lobby and introduced herself as Polina Botkina.

"How did you know who I was?" She smiled and responded, "When you entered through those doors there was little doubt that Bill Bond was your father."

They decided to sit in the lobby to talk before having their dinner. "Could you tell me a little about the time you spent with my father?" She seemed anxious to reply, "Bill Bond was both a charmer and gentleman. He was sent to Chelyabinsk by our agency under contrived charges, and I am still angry with the leadership at the time for subjecting him to house arrest without him being able to communicate with his loved ones."

She went on to explain that the house they were domiciled in was the house where Joseph Stalin's mistress Alyesa Ivanova lived for many years. She told Vasily about their good times watching old Hitchcock movies, exercising together, and how he taught her so many basics about ballroom dancing.

"And now I want to tell you a secret that was strictly between your father and I. When he first arrived I cautioned him there would be no physical contact (sexual) between us and we adhered to that principle although I must admit that both of us wanted to be in the same bed together. I had lost my husband Alex in a boat accident a few years earlier and your father treated me with the utmost respect. I would take two week vacation breaks during the 14 months we were together.

Your father was a great dancer and while on one of my breaks I took an intensive ten day course learning the bolero. When I returned I dressed in my revealing red dress and panties, cleared enough space to create a dance floor, put on the music to Ravel's bolero, and after about 15 minutes into the dance as our bodies became one I pressed my vulva against his most sensitive part and he had an intense climatic reaction." At this time, both Vasily and Polina could not stop laughing. When they regained their composure she continued;

"I know that you and I are mature enough that we can both look on this with a good amount of levity. At the time, I had to assist him to the couch where he went into a multi-hour slumber. And now I want to hear how you learned that Bill Bond was your father."

Vasily explained that his mother had kept it a secret for almost 43 years, but with just several months to live and her husband Vitali, the man he believed to be his birth father, now deceased, she made the decision that it was best that he know. They moved their conversation from the lobby into the restaurant and Vasily asked, "Did you ever re-marry after you lost your husband in that tragic accident?"

"No I never did and I must confess to you I loved Alex with all my heart but your father helped me through a very emotional time in my life. In fact, even though there was this great age disparity, there were times after he left Chelyabinsk I wondered if I could survive without him." At this time tears began to form in her eyes, as happened so many years ago when she stood on the train depot platform before Bill Bond's departure for Moscow.

"As a matter of fact, I think we were both in love but neither had the courage to admit it to the other." Vasily took her hand and gave her a gentle kiss and hug and as they finished their dinner. Their time together was ending and he reminded her that he was an amateur masseur and if she ever wanted his services he would be at her beckon call. "Tonight is not good for me but I will definitely accept your offer at some future time." He walked her to her car and returned to the hotel to get a room for the evening deciding to wait until morning to drive back to Yaroslavi.

He was amazed that his father was able to attract so many young, beautiful, and talented ladies in the autumn of his years. In the case of Ms. Botkina they were brought together by circumstances that neither had any control over, but it was apparent after his meeting with her this evening, they had bonded in such a way that both had great respect for each other. She was probably in her early 20's when his father and her did their sensual bolero and Vasily could not keep the smile off his face just thinking what it must have been like when Polina realized he was having an event.

The next morning he drove back to Yaroslavi and began to search the internet for possible CEO candidates to run the company that he started just six years earlier. He first went to the magazine, "Russian Business" and under the heading, "Top 100 Executives in Russia"; He couldn't help but notice the name Sergey Petrov who was employed at Gazprom. He remembered that Arno had mentioned a person by that name as being the son of Vera Petrova. When he turned to the page there was a short biography with this information:

Sergey Petrov---Age: 38---Place of birth: St. Petersburg, Russia---School history: Graduate of The London Business School at Regents Park--- Place of employment: Gazprom---Parents: Son of Vera Petrova, now deceased.

He didn't have to read any further, he was sure this was the son of the woman his father intended to marry. It would be the irony of all ironies if Sergey would be taking his place as CEO of the Company that Bill Bond's son had founded. It was almost too bizarre to contemplate but now his top priority was to pick up the phone and dial in Gazprom's central number.

The woman who answered the phone immediately connected him to the extension of Sergey Petrov's office. When his secretary answered, Vasily identified himself as the owner of The Sokolov Cement and Concrete Corporation. She said that Mr. Petrov had stepped out of the office for a minute so they chatted for a while saying she was a friend of a lady who worked out of his Moscow office.

"Yes, I know her well she is a wonderful lady and a very competent employee. You are very fortunate to have her as a friend and I am sure she feels the same about you."

"Mr. Petrov is back now it was nice talking to you." His voice was strong and his delivery was the style of man who possessed great confidence.

"Hello, this is Sergey Petrov, how can I help you?" Vasily didn`t know whether his secretary had written his name down and given it to him so he introduced himself and then posed this question, "Is the name Bill Bond familiar to you?" After a few seconds, "Yes, there was a man by that name that was to marry my mother prior to her dreadful accident that ended her life. I never met him personally since I was attending school in London at the time he was dating my mum. She told me he was the kindest, most generous man she had ever met."

Any small doubt Vasily may have had about his identity was now completely erased. "If I told you Bill Bond was my biological father what would you think?"

After a long pause, "If you say you are I have no reason not to believe you." After a while they became very comfortable with each other and they arranged a meeting at Vasily`s facility in Yaroslavl for the 5th of next month at 10a.m.

All the pieces were beginning to come together and now at least for the next few weeks he would have time to relax and reflect. Vasily felt he could begin to plan his future now. He was confident he had done all he could to be sure that his corporation would continue to prosper, after his day to day duties were consummated. He would not even consider another prospective candidate to take his place until after his meeting with Sergey Petrov.

Ambush in Islamabad

It was late in the evening when he picked up the Moscow Times and noticed a story by much decorated correspondent Svetlani Cheranova. It was not only a noteworthy article but it had a sad personal touch for Svetlani as well. Four CIA operatives had been gunned down in Pakistan as they were attempting to intercept terrorists who had plans to send two suicide bombers on to the grounds of the American Embassy in Islamabad. The bombers were stymied from completing their mission, but as he read further he saw the name Ben Stevens, as being one of the deceased, and his stomach turned into knots. All the plans for his future did not prepare him for this. Svetlani went on to write that Ben Stevens wife Olga Kornakova was a precious friend of hers.

It had been nearly seven years since Olga had been right here in this very room sitting in the chair he had christened, "My chair for honored guests only." It was his mother Galina's favorite chair and when she passed away it became one of his prized possessions. Now, all he could think about was Olga and her daughters Marina and Anastasia as he sat down and wrote a short electronic letter telling her he was here for her if he could help in anyway. Vasily understood it was no time for him to enter into her life at this time. There would be a long period of mourning for family and close friends on both sides.

But he could never forget how much Olga meant to him. She sacrificed so much to help him gain his dual citizenship. He would now wait until this tragedy that affected so many had allowed enough time to pass for the healing process to begin. Of course, when you lose someone so unexpectedly while still in the prime of one's life the scars never completely heal. But for those still left behind, when something of this magnitude strikes, life must go on and so it was for him.

The day had arrived for his 10a.m meeting with Sergey Petrov and he was right on time. Vasily`s first impression of him was very positive. An upright posture, with a gait that exuded confidence, it was obvious by his lean and mean body, that he was engaged in some weight lifting program. They shook hands, and looked each other in the eye, leaving little doubt they had an immediate trust and respect for each other.

Vasily knew his business credentials were impeccable but the way he conducted his personal life was even more important. Sergey explained he had been married for 14 years to a lady by the name of Yelena and they had two children, a boy and girl ages twelve and 10. He explained that Yelena was a stay at home mum who enjoyed cooking and baking as well as making the clothes for her children. One of her favorite chores was to go to the vegetable kiosk every day to make sure her dumplings and cabbage soup had the freshest ingredients.

"And by the way she bakes a variety of Russian breads and her dark rye is an award winner and when you come to Moscow you will have to be our guest one evening when she serves her bread with cabbage soup and "pigs in the blanket.""

Vasily responded, "I will certainly keep that in mind but my hope is that you will accept the offer I am about to propose to you and maybe your wife can prepare the dinner right here in your new home in Yaroslavi."

At this time, Vasily handed him a sheet of paper spelling out what his starting salary and bonuses would be. One of the perks would be a rent free home in an upscale Yaroslavi neighborhood and if he remained with the company for ten years the house would be his and Yelena`s with a clear and free title. Sergey studied the offer for no more than fifteen minutes at which time he stood up and extended his hand.

"Sir, I accept your offer and I can start as early as 60 days from today. That is considered a fair amount of time that Gazprom needs to find a replacement."

With the death of Ben Stevens still heavy on his mind having a replacement for himself would give him the time to take care of personal matters. He wanted to be sure that Sergey knew more about his new quarters.

"I purchased the house and property last year. I fell in love with the rare Gothic design, and the existing kitchen was spacious so your wife with her many cooking and baking skills should have ample space. I upgraded all the kitchen equipment and redid the bathrooms. I hope both of you will love it as much as I do. Also, during the 60 day waiting period Ms. Petrova is more than welcome to go by the house anytime, and see what changes she might want to make, as well as choosing the colors and wallpaper for the various rooms. In fact, I will be happy to meet her there along with my interior decorator if she likes. Here are two sets of keys and if you want to go by on your way home to take a look feel free to do so."

With that, they shook hands and as Vasily drove back home he knew he had made the right choice. It all seemed so unimaginable that Sergey, the son of the woman who his birth father was prepared to marry, before her fateful accident, would one day run the company he had founded. Of course Bill Bond had no idea when he came to St. Petersburg to marry Vera Petrova, he had a 32 year old son living in Moscow by the name of Vasily Sokolov.

Nearly three weeks had passed since Ben Stevens and three of his comrades were ambushed in Pakistan when he received a short e-mail from Olga: "Dear Vasily, thanks so much for your kind offer of assistance. Right now, I am still in a state of disbelief and confusion. My finances are in good shape because the CIA always kept a special fund for those killed in the line of duty which is quite generous. Since he was near retirement age I will also have a nice income. If you ever visit near the Washington, D.C. area maybe we can get together for dinner and conversation. As Always, Olga"

It seemed as if she was coping with this tragedy quite well and with her finances in good shape it will at least lift that burden from her shoulders. Of course he was more than able and ready to assist her in that regard if necessary, but being a proud and independent woman it was probably a route she would rather not take.

Ron Brown of Morgan Stanley called the next morning informing him that the documents and paperwork were now prepared for the transfer of his company from a sole ownership to an employee owned entity. Vasily informed Ron he had found a very capable CEO to replace himself. He decided not to divulge that Sergey's mother was the woman his biological father intended to marry, before her unfortunate accident. Vasily, agreed to fly to New York in two weeks, to make official, the transfer of ownership.

Love at First Sight

Meanwhile, Yelena Petrova, the wife of his new CEO called to say she would be happy to accept his offer to meet with him, and the interior decorator at their future home in Yaroslavi. It was just a three hour drive from her present home on the outskirts of Moscow and they agreed to a 2p.m meeting three days hence. Vasily decided to travel to London after that meeting and spend some time in Western Europe prior to his meeting in New York with Ron Brown. Perhaps he could arrange a dinner engagement with Dasha Brumel in Paris in that time frame.

But now, the day arrived when he would meet with Yelena Petrova, the wife of the new CEO, at the house where she and Sergey would reside when he assumed his new position. After taking care of all his morning chores he drove over to pick up Igor, his contractor, for their afternoon appointment.

Now and then in life, you meet someone so impressive, they "knock you off your feet" in the first hour you meet them. Such was the case with Yelena Petrova. She was a real sweetheart with a beguiling smile, piercing hazel eyes, fiery red hair and a personality that could disarm the most seasoned drill sergeant.

From the moment she stepped out of her car she left little doubt that she was in charge as she led Vasily and Igor from room to room. "What is our budget limit?" Without trying to say there was no actual budget limit Vasily responded, "Try to keep it under 100 million rubles." However, it was apparent she was budget conscience asking Igor about the difference in prices regarding products that would be required to make the changes and additions she thought were necessary. For the cabinets she wanted to add in the kitchen, she chose Russian oak rather than the more expensive Canadian and Australian imports.

Igor assured her that he could obtain all the necessary materials locally and would be able to complete the work before her move in date. As they walked her to her car she expressed how much she liked the house and property and couldn't wait to move in. She gave them both a big hug and gentle kiss and although in some circles this might be considered improper, it fit her warm personality and didn't seem unusual at all. As Vasily and Igor drove away they both agreed they had met a very special lady and wondered why she had not aspired to be a professional person rather than a traditional Russian house wife.

After dropping Igor off at his office he continued on to Moscow to catch the evening flight to London. He would spend two days there at the Grosvenor House and then take the Eurostar Chunnel train to Paris where he had reserved a room at the Four Seasons Hotel where he would be meeting Dasha Brumel at the hotel restaurant.

But, with all these places to visit, along with his trip to New York to take the final step to turn over his corporation to his employees, he could only think of Yelena Petrova. It made him look back to the time he married Magdalina, when she chose a career path instead of having children, and maybe, even, be a stay at home mum. Although he had spent less than two hours with her, It was obvious that Yelena was a woman of great intellect, and with all her other talents, she could have succeeded in any field she chose. So, with all his wealth and at 50 years of age he was missing the things he wanted most, a loving wife and children. At age 38, Sergey Petrov, had everything, an adorable wife, two lovely children, and now he would be CEO of a very successful and profitable company.

It wasn't a matter of envy, because Vasily was happy to have been able to recruit Sergey, and when he met Yelena, it was like hitting the jackpot twice in the same week. Although he had not met their two children he could only imagine they inherited all the superior qualities of their parents.

A Trip to London and Paris

When his plane touched down at Heathrow he immediately took a taxi to the Grosvenor House. His main reason for wanting to spend some time in London was to visit the Islington Borough in Greater London where Vladimir Lenin (aka: Vladimir Ilyich Uylanov) spent a year in 1902-03. In his leisure time, Vasily studied Russian history and of course Lenin was probably the most notable of all in the 20th century. So, the next morning he hired a taxi for the entire day and lucky for him the driver was very familiar with the history of the area. He was able to point out the structure where Lenin, Marta, Krupskaya and other Russian dissidents lived in a communal style setting.

They visited the Crown Tavern in Clerkenwell where legend has it that Lenin met Joseph Stalin for the first time. They then drove to Primrose Hill, which Lenin loved, because not only could you get a good view of London but it was also the location of the Highgate Cemetery where Karl Marx was buried. Lenin admired Marx who was known as the father of socialism and wrote the Communist Manifesto which Lenin studied with intense vigor. Lenin loved to read and he spent much of his time in the London Library where he was actually employed for a short time. The day had gone by so quickly and there were other places he wanted to visit so he hired the taxi for the next day.

Lenin liked the Hyde Park area of London because here is where the orators of the time would come to deliver either their religious sermons or their socialist and atheist views. He would listen to them and actually study their lips to have a better understanding of the English language. The next morning, Vasily would be taking the Eurostar train to Paris. He understood he would be coming back to London in the future because there were so many historical places to visit. In a few months he would have time to visit many cities when he would begin his retirement.

The next morning he boarded the Eurostar train that would take him under the English Channel for the two hour trip to Paris. This was the best way to travel between London and Paris since it took you to the central part of both cities. The actual time to traverse the distance under the channel itself, seemed less than twenty five minutes but it is a trip well worth the time for any visitor.

When Vasily arrived, he got a taxi to The Four Seasons Hotel where he would be spending the next several days. He was fortunate because he was able to secure the services of Melisse, the taxi lady for the trip to the Versailles Palace and Museum the next day. He would be meeting with Dasha Brumel this evening for dinner at the hotel restaurant. He had exchanged e-mails with her some weeks ago, and she touched upon the relationship she had with his father Bill Bond, when she was Deputy Commander of the RIS in St. Petersburg. He went to the hotel jewelry outlet and purchased a friendship bracelet, although sometime ladies are reluctant to accept a gift, thinking the guy is trying to soften her emotions before inviting her to his room. Nevertheless, since she knew his father so well he reasoned it was the proper thing to do.

When he got to his room (more like a suite) he immediately sent Ms. Brumel an e-mail reminding her of their 7pm dinner engagement and she quickly responded that she was looking forward to it. He then went down to the restaurant to alert the manager and reserve a table. He requested that a dozen red roses be delivered to their table right after their drink selections. At the Four Seasons this is the kind of services to expect and of course it will be added to your tab at checkout.

He had brought the sport coat that his ex-wife Magdalina had purchased for him before going to dinner at the Taleon in St. Petersburg and he would wear it tonight. When he was married to her she would always choose his dress clothes because it was a chore he did not relish. But now, it was time to go back downstairs and he would wait for her arrival in the restaurant vestibule. He had guessed she would be in her late 40's and after looking up information from her days in the RIS and seeing her picture posted he understood she would be a most beautiful lady.

But spectacular would be a better word as a lady wearing a blue low cut dress entered and looked right at him with a most compelling smile, "Hi Mr. Sokolov you look so much like your father."

He stood up and they embraced as if they were the best of friends as the hostess led them to their reserved table. He had alerted the manager that they would be in no hurry for their entries after their drinks and roses were delivered. He wanted ample time for conversation. They had both chosen Russian champagne and since it was known to have aphrodisiac qualities maybe it was a good omen for what might follow.

When the roses were delivered she stood up and went to his chair to give him an appreciative hug. They had so much to talk about and she anticipated what his questions might be so she got the conversation off the ground.

"As I told you in my letter, your father and I did spend some time together in St. Petersburg going to dinner, visiting museums, going out to Peterhoff and just walking at times in the park. Yes, we did spend some intimate hours together in my bedroom suite and I make no apologies to anyone since we were both unattached at the time.

When I assumed my official duties there I had little time for leisure activities since I was up to my eyeballs just trying to get adjusted to the awesome responsibilities in my new position. Bill and I exchanged e-mails for a time but he was travelling from city to city and we just kind of lost touch. About a year into my new job I met a man whom I believed was worthy of consideration for possible marriage in the future since we had so many common interests such as skiing, hiking, biking, etc. One of our favorite vacation places was in Lucerne, Switzerland where we could be close to our favorite slopes at Mt. Titlis." Before continuing, it was obvious she was getting emotional as she picked up her champagne glass and drank what remained. Bill told her she didn't have to go any further but she insisted.

"On one of our vacations there, I was going to be delayed for a day so he went ahead to get our villa stocked and ready. When my appointment was cancelled I got their early and found him in bed with another person. Whether man or woman it didn't matter because it was the last time I would ever be with him. Later, I got the position in Moscow I had always wanted but after two years I was exhausted and as my thirty years in the RIS was ending I decided to retire. After a few months of retirement I was offered a prestigious position at the World Bank, which I accepted, because it would be a challenge and living in Paris seemed exciting and invigorating. It worked out well because I love my job and I love Paris."

It took Vasily a few minutes to digest everything he had just listened to and yes her recitation answered almost all the questions he had in my mind and all he could think to say was, "Thanks a million for alerting Polina Botkina that I would be contacting her. She is such a delightful lady and perhaps she told you of our dinner meeting at the Radisson Park Hotel in Moscow."

This brought a smile to Dasha's face when she gave Vasily this reminder, "Yes, she also told me you were a masseur and promised to give her a massage some evening in the future." Vasily paused for a moment before responding, "Yes, I did offer my services, and when I return to Moscow I will contact her and arrange a meeting."

The server appeared at this time and asked if they were ready for their entries which had been ordered in advance. Both agreed they were hungry enough, and when the waiter left to alert the kitchen, Vasily thought it was a good time to give her the friendship bracelet he had purchased earlier. Not knowing what her reaction would be he nevertheless removed it from his pocket and presented it to her. "Vasily, you are so much like your father in every way, first the beautiful roses, and now this precious bracelet. If they were meant to lure me to your bedroom I accept."

Her offer took him by complete surprise because these small gestures were not meant to have such a profound effect. But it was just what he needed to deal with his constant thoughts of Yelena Petrova and maybe a woman's love would be good therapy. Besides, Dasha was a very attractive and desirable lady.

"If you are serious my room is very spacious and my bed is quite comfortable." She gave him a most beguiling smile and then suggested, "I am most serious but let us enjoy our entries and dessert so that our energy level will be good."

He was already feeling the effects of her offer and he realized he was eating too quickly not giving his digestive system much of a break. She understood his dilemma by reminding him that the rewards are always greater for those who are patient. When they had completed their meal she went to her car to get her overnight bag and as he waited in the lobby he could hardly control his emotions. They took the elevator to his suite on the third floor and upon entering he offered her the combination bath and dressing room while he took the small bathroom. When he got his shower and put on his night shirt she appeared a few minutes later in her bikini style red panties and bra. She was beautiful beyond description and as he took her hand and led her to his bed he removed her bra and panties kissing her rounded breasts and kneeling to kiss her vulva before carefully lifting her up and placing her gently on his bed.

He began to massage her body with cocoa oil and her face flushed to an orange glow letting Vasily know that the enjoyment she was experiencing was more than she could possibly imagine. At this time he moistened her vagina and entered and this was truly a heaven on earth experience for both.

They fell asleep in tight embrace and when he awoke the next morning he remembered that he had a 10a.m appointment with Melisse, his taxi lady for his trip to Versailles. It was now 7:30am and as they showered together he invited Dasha to come with him to Versailles and she accepted with enthusiasm knowing it was her day off. Although just 20 kilometers from Paris she had never visited this historic venue. They got dressed and went downstairs to have a light breakfast. She then drove over to her town house to get into some proper attire and would be back by 9:45.

During the drive there, Melisse filled them in with some history of the Grand Palace and Museum going back to the middle of the 16th century when Louis the 13th first purchased some land there for a hunting lodge. The grand opening was in 1642, and Louis 14[th,] actually began to move the Royal Family from Paris to the Court of Versailles, and it remained the seat of power until the French Revolution in 1789 forced them to move back to Paris. When they arrived it was an awesome and inspiring structure and they learned it consisted of 2300 rooms and over 6000 paintings.

Melisse instructed them on how to start their tour and would be back in five hours for the return trip to Paris. Vasily and Dasha were still thinking of their evening together the night before and as they walked together from room to room, marveling at what they were viewing, they would stop now and then to embrace almost as if they were newlyweds. Being here made you feel as if you were sharing time with all the great artisans of the past. As they sat down to have lunch at the Palace cafeteria Dasha could not help but to smile offering this thought, "If your father, Bill Bond, had known he had a Russian son that would one day share a bed with me as he had done I wonder what he might be thinking."

They both agreed he would have probably given both of them his blessing. Their day at Versailles was ending and it would be an unforgettable experience. They had climbed a lot of stairs and looked at hundreds of paintings and they both expressed a desire to re-visit one day because there was so much more here to see and enjoy. When they got back to the Four Seasons they were exhausted and Dasha having to go back to work tomorrow, and Vasily going back to London, they embraced and promised to share more time together in the future.

The next morning Melisse took him to the Eurostar terminal for his trip back to London. During the two hour ride he began to think how fortunate he was when his mother divulged to him that his biological father was Bill Bond. He loved his Russian papa Vitali but the revelation by his mum opened so many doors. He would have never met Olga, Dasha, Polina, Arno or even his future CEO Sergey Petrov and his lovely wife Yelena without her disclosure. By obtaining dual citizenship he was able to secure the 22 million dollar loan from Morgan Stanley to start his business. It was so successful that now, just six years after the first shovel of dirt was turned, he would be signing papers in the morning that would transfer ownership to his employees.

When he arrived in London, he had just several hours to get to Heathrow. His time with Dasha was extra special. She was a woman of great passion and conviction. Lucky for her, her trip to Lucerne finding her possible future husband in bed with another person, she was able to avoid an episode in her life with possible career ending consequences. As he boarded his plane for New York his mind was filled with shifting thoughts. As soon as he was airborne he dozed off, not awakening until the steward announced they would be landing at JFK in 25 minutes.

Ron Brown was waiting for him in the terminal reception area and after the handshakes they got into his company car, and drove to the Morgan Stanley offices. In one hour the deal was consummated and the company he founded, now with an estimated worth of 400 million dollars, belonged to his employees. It was also a million dollar payday for Ron Brown and a five million dollar fee for Morgan Stanley.

He was happy for both Ron and his company because without their hard work and planning and the original 22 million dollar loan his company may have never been able to sprout its wings. He would stay over in New York for only one night because he still had the responsibility of interim CEO until Sergey Petrov took over which was still over a month away.

When he got back to Moscow, he received an e-mail from Igor, his contractor, saying he had completed all the changes and additions Yelena Petrova had requested in her future home. Vasily was very happy to hear this since it give him an opportunity to contact Yelena and possibly have her visit the house to inspect the work. He was so anxious to see her and although he understood he was treading in dangerous territory with such strong feelings, for the wife of the future CEO, he could not pass up the opportunity to see her again. So he sat down and penned this e-mail to her;

"Dear Ms. Petrova, Igor has informed me that he has completed all the work you requested at your future new home. He and I will be happy to meet you there at any time. Also, although your husband still has approximately one month before he assumes his duties at his new company feel free to move in early if you wish, respectfully yours, Vasily Sokolov."

He also alerted Igor to be prepared to allow some time on his schedule over the next week in case she accepts his offer for a meeting. In other words, try to stay in the vicinity of the Yaroslavi Oblast. Igor got a good percentage of his work from Vasily and he immediately responded he would be available at whatever time or day he specified. Not long after hearing from Igor he received this e-mail;

"Dear Mr. Sokolov: You are such a kind and considerate person and I will gladly accept your offer to meet you and Igor at the property and while there, I can put some of our winter clothes in the closets as well as stock some items in the kitchen pantry. Any afternoon in the next three days would be good for me. Thank you very much. Love, Yelena."

When he received her e-mail he was stunned by her ending. He had only met her one other time and it seemed a little too personal when she added the word "love." But on the other hand, it fit her personality perfectly. He remembered the affectionate hugs he and Igor got when they met her a month ago. To read anything into it other than she was just being herself would be unfair and stupid on his part. Nevertheless, when he responded to set a time and day for their meeting, he would sign off similarly, because in truth, he was really in love with her. The quickness of his feelings for her made everything seem so bizarre and unreal.

His father, Bill Bond, had fallen in love with Vera Petrova after meeting her for the first time according to Arno, the taxi driver in St. Petersburg. Now, several decades later he falls in love with a woman with the same surname who happens to be the wife of Vera Petrova's son. But Bill Bond and Vera Petrova were both unattached at the time and Yelena is presumably happily married with two children. Yet, he seems helpless to stop himself from doing something that is so irresponsible.

So he alerts Igor that he will set up an appointment with Ms. Petrova and then sends this e-mail:

"Dear Yelena…Igor and I will be happy to meet you on Thursday at 2pm if it is o.k. with you. Love, Vasily"

As soon as he sent it he felt he had acted too boldly but shortly after she responded: "Dear Vasily, I will be looking forward to seeing you again. Love, Yelena"

He interpreted her response to mean that they had reciprocal feelings for each other. He understood the possible implications for the three adults and the two children, Nada and Pavel. It would be less than a month when her husband would be assuming his new duties as CEO of the Sokolov Cement and Concrete Corporation. If he and Yelena were to meet in secret in the future to have a physical relationship, and it was discovered, people would believe that was his reason for recruiting Sergey in the first place.

Of course this would not be true since he had not met Yelena until many days after Sergey had accepted his offer. As Thursday approached for their 2pm appointment he was happy that Igor would also be there. After their exchange of e-mails, he understood he may not have the will power to constrain himself from embracing her, in such a way, that their emotions may take them to the next logical action, if they were in the house alone. A scandal is never good but a scandal this close after he had just signed over his company to his employees would bring out the conspiratorial brigade in all its fury.

As he lay in bed on Wednesday evening he began to think of other scandals or near scandals he had read about. The founder of McDonalds, Ray Kroc, had fallen in love with a piano player at a bar in St. Paul, Minnesota while both were married. They carried on a secret affair for 12 years before divorcing their spouses and getting married. Yet, when the public learned of this, McDonalds continued to grow in leaps and bounds.

Then there was the scandal in the United Kingdom where Edward, the Prince of Wales, was having an affair with Wallis Simpson who was married at the time. When Edward's father, King George the 5th, suddenly passed away he ascended to the throne and continued to see Mrs. Simpson for sexual trysts. When the public learned he was having an affair with a woman with two ex-husbands who were still alive, a constitutional crisis ensued and Edward abdicated the throne to marry "the woman that I love."

But this was Russia, and although having a mistress was still considered a status symbol in some circles, the old Russia when Alexander Pushkin had several mistresses was no longer the norm. Vasily remembered when he interviewed Sergey and learned that he and Yelena had been married for 14 years. Perhaps Sergey had a mistress or two during those years and now she would act on the emotions she had constrained so long.

Of course this was only conjecture on his part. With all those thoughts racing through his mind he must not have slept at all because the sun had peeked through his bedroom shutters and when he looked at his clock it was now 7a.m. This afternoon, he would pick up Igor, and they would drive over to meet with Yelena. When he poured his morning cup of coffee he spilled half of it on the tile floor and there was little doubt he was already nervous with the anticipation of seeing her again.

After making all his morning calls and sent out all his e-mails it was now time to pick up Igor. When he arrived at Igor's office he could not help but notice he looked different. He had shaved off his beard and dressed in his best clothes. "Igor, we are not going to attend a wedding, we are just going over to meet with Ms. Petrova." Igor smiled before responding, "I want to show her great respect because she is without a doubt one of the classiest ladies I have ever met. I am nervous because I am not sure she will be satisfied with all my work." Vasily understood when she had that kind of effect on a tough contractor like Igor she had to be someone very special. After all, Igor had performed work on many upscale homes in Yaroslavi and met some high class ladies but he had never shaved off his beard until now.

When they arrived at 1:45pm Yelena was already there walking the grounds. It was a glorious day in May, she was wearing a one piece, low cut dress of pink and white, and with her mesmerizing smile and dark red hair she was the epitome of seductive beauty and gentle grace. He remembered Sergey had told him she made all the clothes for her and the kids, and it was obvious the dress she was wearing was tailor-made leaving little doubt what was underneath. When she spotted them she trotted over and gave each a genuine embrace. As they entered the house exchanging pleasantries, she went right to the kitchen heaping praise on Igor for the craftsmanship of the custom made Russian oak cabinets. As they walked from room to room she continued to shower Igor with superlatives for his workmanship.

A Gesture from Yelena

When they opened the door to enter the master bedroom suite Vasily was awe struck. It was not only the stunning blue wallpaper that caught his eye but interspersed in the design were nude figures of all the Greek gods and goddesses leaving nothing to the imagination. Of course this was Yelena's choice and she again heaped praise on Igor asking him to pass on her thanks and appreciation to the craftsmen he had chosen to do the work. This bedroom suite was designed to get you in the mood and Vasily was feeling it from head to toe. Igor excused himself to go to the water closet and like all well trained contractors he went to the one at the lowest level.

Almost spontaneously, Vasily and Yelena embraced with her moving her tongue to his left ear lobe and whispering, "If you are in town next week it will be our opportunity. I will be sending you an e-mail."

Just her words and the movement of her tongue had provided a release and he could not help but embrace her tightly until it was over. Knowing what had just occurred she gave him a smile and touched him there saying, "I am sorry, if Igor were not here I would clean you up. I can't wait until we meet next week when I will provide you with the full service."

When they heard the flushing in the water closet downstairs they began to meander slowly toward the steps as Igor appeared at the bottom. After completing her inspection, they walked to her car giving both men another embrace seeming to give Igor a more spirited one.

He understood that it was Yelena's way of letting him know how pleased she was with all his efforts but also to give the impression he was more special than Vasily. On the way back to Igor's office, both men went on and on about what a wonderful woman she was, with Igor never hinting whether he had noticed anything between him and Yelena. All Vasily could think of was the words she whispered in his ear. "If you are in town next week it will be our opportunity" and his brief climatic experience. The day of decision would soon be here but in reality there was no decision to make. He would eagerly await her e-mail and whatever was to follow, he was helpless to stop even if he was so inclined. It was a spontaneous love they felt for each other from the first few minutes they met and there was little doubt they were powerless to apply any brakes for all that was inevitably to follow.

It would be just over a week when Sergey would begin his new duties so he decided to spend the next few days at the facility to be sure everything was operating at full efficiency so that the transition would be as smooth as possible. Giving up his company and position was bittersweet in many ways. On the one hand freeing him from those long 18 hour days to travel and do the enjoyable things he seldom had time for, on the other hand, he was going to miss all the employees he cared so much about. It was an emotional letdown that only entrepreneurs can understand. In fact, most can't let go staying until the final few years of their lives.

When Monday arrived he checked his e-mails every hour. Surprisingly, he got one from Olga saying she was attending a social group for professionals who had lost their spouses in some untimely event and Judge Jimmy Walker was one of the attendees. Judge Walker had recently lost his wife in a skiing accident in Colorado.

There were so many ironies since Vasily's late mother, Galina, informed him his biological father was Bill Bond. This was just another example and wouldn't it be strange if Olga and the judge ended up tying the proverbial knot. Vasily sent her back a short letter expressing how happy he was that she was taking such a positive step toward her emotional recovery, since the untimely death of her husband Ben Stevens.

A Time of Love and Passion

Later that afternoon he received the e-mail he was so eagerly awaiting. "My Dear Vasily, can you meet me at the house at 1pm tomorrow? I love you very much. Yelena."

Before he could fully adsorb the words he hit the response arrow, "Yes, I can't wait to be with you."

Her words were becoming more expansive and now he understood there would be no turning back. All the things in his mind about past affairs with people like Ray Kroc, King Edward, John Kennedy and Franklin Roosevelt no longer mattered. He was so smitten by Yelena he could not resist her invitation if his very life was in the balance.

It would be 22 hours before their meeting and he decided to drive over to the Ecotel lodge and restaurant at the Romanov Forest to have dinner and get in a few laps at their pool. The drive over and the drive back was like being in some holding pattern while the snow was being removed from the runway below. Before going to bed he watched the Yaroslavi Locomotiv team beat Minsk for the Russian Hockey League championship. He would never forget the horrible airplane accident that wiped out their entire team in 2011 as they headed to Minsk. When he awoke the next morning all his thoughts were consumed thinking of his 1p.m meeting with Yelena.

After passing the morning doing his household chores and gardening it was now time to make that fateful drive and when he arrived Yelena's car was already in the driveway. When he walked up the steps to the front door she opened it and they were in immediate and full embrace. She took him by the hand and led him up the stairs and when she opened the door to the bedroom suite she had made a make shift bed with blankets and a blue cotton sheet that matched the décor of the room.

With the Greek gods and goddesses peering at them from the walls and ceilings she led him over and placed one of the pillows on top of the sheet and knelt down in front of him as she unbuckled his belt. When she removed his briefs she used her tongue and mouth to get his juices flowing. She looked up expressing to him her desire for both to give and receive oral stimulation prior to conventional intercourse. When she arose he removed her bra and used his tongue to lick her rounded breasts before kneeling to remove her panties again using his tongue to stimulate her clitoris. As they slipped onto to the make shift bed she expressed her desire for him to enter her vagina from the rear and it was a favorite position for him also and they both achieved a full and satisfying orgasm almost simultaneously.

This did not end their afternoon as they embraced still getting satisfaction from kissing and touching each other as if they were teen agers. As they lay together she expresses a desire to get something off her mind about her husband Sergey.

"First let me say you could not have found a more qualified and competent CEO than my husband. He is a wonderful family man, and a good example of that, is where he is today. He took Pavel and Nada to St. Petersburg on Sapsan for an overnight trip where Pavel will participate in a junior chess tournament. Nada will act as Pavel's coach and Sergey will be a very proud observer. Both children have won in competitions, sometimes in categories above their age group and Sergey has been their mentor from day one. He is a good husband and great father."

"Sergey and I began to have some problems several years ago when I learned he was having an affair with a woman in Kenya. His passion was big game hunting and she was one of the safari guides. She was of English and native Kenyan descent and when I confronted him he admitted to having sex with her in a very unconventional way which I will not describe to you. It was an African thing."

At this time Yelena began to sob and Vasily tried to comfort her by explaining she did not need to continue. "No, there is more I need to tell you. I never asked him to stop seeing her when he made subsequent trips to Kenya. Yes, I was disgusted with him but I understood his virtues far outweighed his indiscretions of the flesh. And then when I met you for the first time right here at this house I fell in love almost immediately."

At this time they embraced tightly and Vasily began to confess that he too had fallen deeply in love with her. It was now 7pm and the May sun was beginning to set in the western sky when they agreed to meet discreetly and secretly on occasion until some possible resolution in the future. They took their shower together and Vasily remembering his mother being impregnated a half century ago by his father Bill Bond asked if there was a chance this might happen since his release was so strong.

"No, my period ended just 3 days ago and my ovulation begins exactly 11 days later. When we meet in the future I will always make sure the timing is right. If the timing doesn't work we can get our pleasure orally."

With that, they gathered up the make shift bed and got dressed. He walked her to her car as she began the 3 hour trip back to Moscow. As Vasily drove away he was both ecstatic and scared. She inferred they would have similar experiences in the future and the excitement and exhilaration gave him a feeling of fulfillment he had not felt in his entire life. Yet, if discovered, the implications could be enormous. But for now, he would enjoy the memory of this afternoon with the lady he loved so much.

He understood his life had changed in a dramatic way and whether he could make the necessary adjustments for a positive outcome would be a challenge unlike any other he had to undertake in the past. His plans after passing the torch to his successor was to travel to the America's and beyond but now when he travelled it would depend in great part on the 35 year old wife of Sergey Petrov, the man who would succeed him at the Sokolov Cement and Concrete Corporation.

On June 1, Sergey would be taking over and Vasily had retained a catering company in Moscow to prepare a feast for his 200 employees and their families. It would be a welcoming party for the new CEO and in anticipation of this day he had purchased a 4 acre parcel of land just 3 miles from the company facility several years before. It was a two year project installing recreational equipment such as a carousel, picnic benches, tables, barbeque pits, several tennis courts and a covered heated Olympic style swimming pool. It would be the grand opening of the recreational facility and would be there in the future for company parties or a place for families to take their children throughout the year.

When the day arrived it would be an opportunity to see Yelena again and just the thought alone made the blood in his veins flow to every extremity. It was a perfect day for a party as the warm river breeze off the Volga was a hint that summer was just around the corner. The band he hired struck up some traditional Russian music but also some hip-hop and light metal selections more popular in Western Europe and America.

Vasily and Sergey moved through the crowd trying to shake hands with all their employees and family members. Later, Yelena came over and introduced her two children, Pavel and Nada to Vasily. It was apparent from their good manners, excellent postures and choice of words, they had the foundational requirements necessary for future success. Yelena and Vasily hugged and the electricity from the afternoon they had spent together less than a week ago was still very much present. It took every ounce of will power from pulling her into his arms.

The day of celebration was coming to an end and everyone had gotten their fill of roasted pig, baked beans, sauerkraut and sweet potatoes. There were no alcoholic beverages relying on spring water and Arnold Palmer's (combination of lemonade and ice tea) to quench everyone's thirst. And now, the company was officially in the hands of Sergey Petrov, a man he respected and had great confidence in, and whose wife he was madly in love with.

Yes, he was now free to pursue all the plans he had mapped out for himself just six months earlier but that was before he met Yelena and all he could think about was his next meeting with her. It was so silly of him but when she told him her menstrual period was so steady he decided to keep a calendar. He remembered she told him after the last day of her period her ovulation would begin 11 days later lasting no more than six days in a 28 day cycle. Now he could make a good guess as to the time frame when they might get together again.

Just being with her brought him great joy and she mentioned they could derive great pleasure in oral love if the time frame didn't always work out. Today, Sergey and Yelena, along with their children, Pavel and Nada would be moving into their new home. To relax, Vasily decided to take the train to Plyos, a small picturesque village on the Volga River about 2 hours from Yaroslovi. He was hoping it would provide the peace and serenity he was badly in need of to clear his mind.

He was able to get the luxury suite at the Volga-Volga Hotel which provided massage services. Vasily, worn out from all the activities at the company party, took immediate advantage. The pretty Belarusian girl who administered the massage was delightful teasing him with hand movements close to the zone not included in the price. Her name was Inna, and when she didn't have an appointment for her massage service, she would walk or jog with Vasily during his morning exercise routine and he was more than happy to have her company. His time in Plyos went by quickly, and on his last night there, they performed reciprocal conventional massage therapies in the privacy of Vasily's suite.

Time in her Basement Sewing Room

But now, it was time to board the train and return to Yaroslavi and when he arrived at his home he received this e-mail from Yelena. "Dear Vasily, You told me during our afternoon together your father was of English and Irish descent so on Wednesday I am going to make some corn beef and cabbage for the family and I want you to join us. You have not been in our house since we moved in so I want to show you our handiwork. Sergey has many of his big game trophies adorning our walls so I hope you are not offended as some of our friends were in Moscow. Dinner will be at 4:30pm but please come at 3pm so I can show you around. When we go to the basement we will be alone for a few minutes and we can use that time to embrace. Can`t wait to see you. You are a big part of my life. Yelena"

Just the thought of being with her again was intoxicating. And the thought that she had planned a way for a few minutes of embrace filled his mind with excitement and anxiety. He quickly sent her a return e-mail telling her he would be looking forward to her cooking and embrace. His short visit to Plyos was a much needed break after all the festivities connected to the transfer of his company from himself to his employees, and Sergey Petrov taking over as the new CEO. Also, meeting Inna was an unexpected treat and it was nice to know she would be there through the summer and fall season.

But Yelena Petrova consumed all of Vasily`s thoughts. It was now Wednesday and the drive over to her house was a time for reflection and mixed emotions. He wanted to see her so badly, and just the thought he would be in her embrace even for a moment, was like being on an emotional roller coaster. The anticipation alone gave him a rush of adrenalin similar to a runner in the starting blocks waiting for the sound of the gun.

As he parked his car, the smell of cabbage was in the air. It reminded him so much of his childhood when his mother, Galina would prepare so many of his favorites like Russian cabbage borscht, halupkies and choucroute. But today Yelena was preparing corn beef and cabbage, an Irish favorite.

When he knocked on the door, within a few seconds she was standing there in her apron and Russian pony tails, giving him her usual welcoming hug. Not long after, Sergey, Pavel, and Nada came to the front and a healthy distribution of smiles and handshakes followed. They treated Vasily as if he were some long lost favorite uncle which made him feel completely at ease. While Pavel and Nada helped their mother in the kitchen Sergey seemed intent on talking about the possibility of expanding the company he had just taken over about a week ago.

Sergey explained that while working at Gazprom he was working on plans to install a huge natural gas pipe line into the Yekaterinburg-Chelyabinsk area near the Ural Mountains. It was to accommodate the new foreign companies like Caterpillar and Siemens who would need natural gas to not only supply the power for its factories, but to convert the natural gas into LNG for transportation purposes. The infrastructure in the area had to be upgraded with road widening and airport expansion and there would be a need for millions of tons of cement and concrete. During Sergey's last month at Gazprom he visited the area and found that most of the companies in the concrete business were small family entrepreneurs unable to bid for the bigger contracts. A company with the size and reputation of the Sokolov Cement and Concrete Corporation would be more than welcome to set up shop there by the political powers.

By this time Vasily was all ears, because starting a new branch brought out his entrepreneur instincts, and it was obvious Sergey had done his homework well. Although he had just retired from the company he started and owned his enthusiasm overcame his usual step by step approach.

"Sergey, I must say you have lit a fire within my spiritual being and I would like to hear more. Of course, you are the CEO and any final decision on this would be yours and the new employee board of directors. How can I help?"

Sergey was quick to respond, "You can help in two ways for now and that is to use your influence with the board if you think my plan is a responsible one. Secondly, when I was in the Sverdlovsk area, there was a "for sale" sign on a 100 acre tract of land that had a house, and two old concrete trucks, in the driveway. They looked like they were leftovers from the Soviet days so I drove up the long driveway and knocked on the door."

"A man by the name of Anatoly Asimov introduced himself to me and we had a nice rapport. He was about 70 and his wife was deceased and he wanted to move into the new retirement community just being built off the main highway. The resources on that tract were plentiful and when he stated his asking price I thought it was a real bargain. Now Vasily, I need someone with your expertise to go over and look at the tract and talk to Mr. Asimov. Would you consider taking on that task?"

Without even thinking what was on his schedule Vasily responded, "I will leave tomorrow if you want." By this time Yelena came into the great room and announced that dinner was being served. She had placed all the food on a serving table and asked Vasily to lead the way. The smell of the cabbage and the freshly baked black Russian bread gave the house an aroma that he had not experienced in quite a while. After placing portions of cabbage, corn beef, potatoes and carrots on his oversized dinner plate he went over to the huge oak round table and sat on the chair that was designated for him. Nada, using her artistic talent made a ribbon shaped like a bow tie with the words, "Welcome Vasily, our special guest."

The food was delicious beyond description and hardly a word was spoken among them because of their indulgence. When Vasily had finished he used every superlative in his playbook to heap praise on Yelena, telling Sergey and the two children how fortunate they were to have such a talented wife and mother. Of course, she was the woman he also loved and that would be a closely guarded secret, at least for now.

After their feast, Sergey suggested that Pavel and Nada clean off the table and then the three of them engage in a game of chess while Yelena gave Vasily a tour of the house.

"She is especially proud of her new sewing room in the basement so she will probably want to spend some extra time there."

Remembering that Yelena had written to him saying they would have some moments to embrace in the basement, Vasily could not help but wonder if Sergey had given his approval to the arrangement.

First she took him upstairs and when they entered the main bedroom suite, the blue wallpaper with the nude Greek gods and goddesses, gave him a vivid reminder of the afternoon they had spent together here. This time, the Greeks had company, with two snarling lion heads peering down in the vicinity of the Victorian style bed no doubt trophies of Sergey's. When they came to the place on the floor where their makeshift bed had been that afternoon, she teased him by placing her hand on his groin for a split second giving him a smile at the same time.

When they went down to the main level Sergey, Pavel, and Nada were fully involved in the game of chess. Knowing how much concentration is required, Yelena and Vasily slipped quietly down the basement stairs. When they arrived in the area where her sewing room was located she wasted little time, allowing her breasts to be exposed as they embraced. With the movement of his tongue and lips giving equal attention to both nipples while she lowered his trousers and gave him a hand massage. It was all over in a precious few minutes. She then went to the sink to get a hand cloth and towel to clean him up.

They checked each other over carefully before ascending the stairway to the main floor. The chess game was still in full competitive mode when Sergey realized it was time to suspend the game and talk to Vasily a little more about his proposed expansion into the Urals area of Russia. Vasily agreed he would go to the region in the next week to talk to Anatoly Asimov and perhaps even purchase the parcel with his personal funds which he would eventually sell to the Sokolov Corporation at the same price.

As someone once said it is better to have one bird in hand rather than two in the bush and if Sergey needed to wait until board approval both birds might be lost in the process. Upon leaving, Yelena gave him a hug also getting warm handshakes from Nada, Pavel, and Sergey. Vasily again assured Sergey, he would go to the Urals within the week, and report back to him after his conversation with Mr. Asimov. When driving back home he had a feeling of elation and puzzlement. Did Sergey actually know of, and approve the basement meeting with him and Yelena? He remembered Yelena telling him that when Sergey was having his affair with the Kenyan woman he was interested in a certain type of sexual gratification saying it was some African thing.

Did knowing his wife was having some sensual minutes in their basement bring him some sort of satisfaction? After all, Sergey was the one who mentioned that Yelena was so proud of her new sewing room she would probably want to spend some extra time there. And Yelena, in her e-mail a few days earlier, had made a point that they would have some time to embrace in that area of the basement. Was she doing this for his benefit alone or had she been drawn into Sergey's web of unusual behavior? And was she too getting some vicarious pleasure from this as well as being with the man she was in love with?

It would be something to ponder over the ensuing days and weeks but now he would begin to plan his trip to the Urals. Regardless of Sergey's sexual fantasies, he was a man with the energy and drive to lead the Sokolov Cement and Concrete Corporation on a path of sustained growth. And helping him take the first step in that direction would not only be doing Sergey a favor but all the employees in the company that he cared so much about. Yes, Vasily held a 2% part of the corporation but percentages are not important when you are on a mission of love.

He spent the following day making all the arrangements for his trip. On Friday, he would board a flight out of Tonoshna in Yaroslavi for the two hour flight to Koltsova in Yekaterinburg. He arranged for a rental car there and would drive over to the Hyatt Regency Hotel where he had reserved a room for seven days. In addition to talking to Mr. Asimov, he would try to arrange short meetings at the offices of the mayor in Yekaterinburg and Chelyabinsk as a gesture of good faith, and provide them with information regarding his intentions to locate another branch of the Sokolov Cement and Concrete Corporation here.

Vasily Travels to Sverdlovsk

And now, Friday had arrived, and the flight to Yekaterinburg was smooth. His rental car was waiting and his hotel accommodations were fit for the most discriminating guest. Of course it had all the amenities of a modern spa and fitness center as well as a heated pool. It's location on the banks of the Iset River gave you an excellent view of the city. In a way, it was sad to see the "Church on the Blood" because it was at its location where the Ipatiev House once stood. Of course, those familiar with Russian history are aware that Tsar Nicholas 2nd, his family, and entourage were herded into the basement and slaughtered by the Bolsheviks.

But this is the new Russia, a growing, vibrant, fledgling democracy, attracting foreign investments and on the way to providing a better life for all. Yes, there are growing pains and the inequities still exist, but with young talented leaders like Sergey Petrov in the ranks of business, good jobs will get into the pipeline.

Today he would make the 50 kilometer drive to Mr. Asimov's property and it was revealing because it was easy to observe the potential the area had for commercial development. With huge water resources and the new gas pipeline being developed by Gazprom gave the area many advantages for the type of manufacturing facilities being planned. The transportation sectors both here in Russia and worldwide was transitioning from diesel to natural gas and its derivatives such as propane and LNG. Multinational companies like Caterpillar, Siemens, United Technologies and scores of others were purchasing sites for future facilities and factories that would build the trucks, tractors, cars, and locomotives that were now in demand in both the developed and underdeveloped countries on the planet. All this would require millions of tons of cement and concrete and if he could make a deal today it would give the Sokolov Cement and Concrete Corporation an opportunity to gain a foot hold here.

When he arrived at the home and property where Mr. Asimov resided he was lucky enough to observe an elderly man with the hood up on a pickup truck. He drove up the driveway and introduced himself. "Hi my name is Vasily Sokolov, are you Anatoly Asimov.?" When he looked up his hands and face were smudged with an oil-like substance. "Yes, let me go over and get some kerosene and cloth to clean up a little and then we can talk." After the kerosene had done its job he primed the water pump and stuck his head under the gusher of water and dried off. "I am now ready to talk." With that they shook hands and Vasily explained he was here to represent Sergey Petrov who had visited him about six weeks earlier. "Oh yes, I remember him well, the nice young man who worked for Gazprom. Come in the house and I will make a pot of coffee where we can sit and talk comfortably."

Vasily recognized quickly he was dealing with a man he liked a lot. He was a down-to-earth gentleman that reminded him of his step father Vitali Sokolov. He expressed his interest in purchasing the property but would need to get a good look at it first.

"I would gladly take you around and show it to you but my truck is not running now."

Vasily suggested they could use his rental van and it didn't take him long to realize that this property was a natural for a cement and concrete company. There was an underground aquifer with an unlimited water supply and a stone and lime quarry close by. Vasily, understanding its intrinsic and strategic location and value made an offer on the spot.

"I will give you your asking price and a 20% premium if we can make a deal today. I can write you out a check for 50% of the full amount now with the remainder after the paperwork is finalized."

It was apparent that Anatoly was having a difficult time digesting his offer. "Are you telling me that I could go to the bank today and cash your check for that amount of money?"

Vasily not only assured him it was possible but told him he would be glad to take him there in his rental van. Anatoly accepted and they went to his house to sign a preliminary contract that Vasily had brought with him. When they got to the bank Anatoly opened up an account and deposited all the funds except enough to purchase a new truck.

Vasily then took him to the truck dealership where he was able to find the vehicle he had coveted for months. Before Anatoly drove it home, they shook hands and hugged, both understanding it was a throwback to the times when there was so much respect for each other, that only a handshake was required to seal a deal. On the drive back to the Hyatt Regency, Vasily began to sing one of his favorite songs he remembered right after he was fluent in English some 35 years ago. "I give you all my love so tenderly."

Of course he was thinking of Yelena Petrova while singing and when he arrived back at the hotel he would have to e-mail her husband, Sergey, and give him the good news about his land purchase. They could now put serious plans in place for the first major expansion of the Sokolov Cement and Concrete Corporation. Sergey was ecstatic when he heard the news and invited Vasily over to his house for dinner upon his return to Yaroslavi to discuss the issue of expansion in private before presenting it to the Board of Directors. Vasily agreed it was a good idea to keep it private for now and accepted the invitation. Of course in the back of his mind it would also be an opportunity to see and perhaps even spend a few minutes in private with Yelena.

But for now, he would need to spend a few more days in the area to get introduced to the bureaucracies here. Zoning should not be a problem since there were already many businesses along that stretch that were similar such as sand & gravel, soil & sod, etc. Everyone he met during the ensuing days was very helpful and cooperative and he felt his trip had accomplished everything and more to get the show on the road, so to speak, for Sergey's expansion plans.

While still in the Sverdlovsk region he was able to go to the property in Chelyabinsk where his father Bill Bond was held under house arrest over two decades earlier. Polina Botkina was his overseer at the time, and he remembered he had promised her a massage at some future date when they dined at The Radisson Hotel in Moscow. He would need to contact her on his return to arrange a time and place to perform this service. The house was converted into a library and he was able to walk through where there seemed to be a full array of selections of Russia's past history from both Russian and western authors. His week had passed quickly and on his drive back to Yekaterinburg he stopped to say goodbye to Anatoly Asimov. His new truck was in the driveway and he said he put a down payment on his new apartment and was looking forward to moving in the next few months. When Vasily arrived back at the Hyatt Regency he called the airline to reserve his seat for the next day for his return trip to Yaroslavi.

On his flight back the next morning he began to reflect on all that happened with his life since he learned Bill Bond was his biological father. He was 43 at the time and now 7 years later he was grateful that his mother Galina made the revelation because without that knowledge he would not have met so many wonderful people.

There was Olga Kornakova, who was willing to sacrifice so much to help him obtain his dual citizenship. His thoughts turned to their time together here in Russia during her visit in the summer of 2027. And of course the memorable massage in the cabin at the Romanov forest. Then, the unimaginable circumstances of Olga's husband Ben Steven's death in Islamabad.

His trip to St. Petersburg where he met Arno that led to his meeting with Dasha Brumel and their time in Paris and Versailles was also in his memory bank as his plane touched down in Yaroslavi.

It was time to shift his thinking to the business at hand. Sergey had mentioned getting together at his house for dinner to discuss how to proceed with their plans for expansion. It was 12 noon when he arrived at his home and when he checked his mails he received two surprising and shocking e-mails. Olga had written saying she was now engaged to Judge Jimmy Walker and they set a wedding date for June of next year with a specific time and place still undetermined. He was happy for her because with her daughters Marina and Anastasia, now in their teens it would provide some stability. Of course he was the Judge who ruled favorably when he applied for dual-citizenship and that is when Olga met him for the first time.

The second e-mail was from Yelena and it was the real shocker. "My Dearest Vasily, You will never know how much I missed you over the past week. Sergey asked me to line up a day to invite you to dinner so the two of you can discuss business. I was hoping you could come Friday. Sergey has an important meeting at the facility at 4:30 p.m. so I am planning dinner for 7. I was hoping you could be here by 2:00 p.m. so we could spend a few hours together alone while Sergey is still at the facility. Nada and Pavel left for summer camp in Germany yesterday and they will be there for a month. Please write me back as soon as you can. You mean everything to me. Yelena"

Wow!!! The implications of her letter meant that they would have several hours for love making before Sergey got home. He maintained a calendar of her menstrual period and Friday would be the second day of her ovulation cycle so no doubt intercourse without a condom will not be in the cards. Or maybe it will be a time for oral love only. What will Sergey think when he finds he had spent several hours with her before his arrival? But he could not resist her tempting offer so he sent back a note saying he would be there at 2pm sharp on Friday. He remembered that Sergey seemed to facilitate their moment of love last time he had dinner there and maybe he was part of this arrangement.

Vasily had great respect for both Sergey and Yelena but sometime human emotions can be so overwhelming that all other considerations are quickly abandoned. Whatever Yelena had planned for him on Friday he was helpless to resist because his love for her was too great.

In the meantime, he would put together a business plan for Sergey to consider when they meet on Friday evening. He would call Ron Brown at Morgan Stanley to alert him to set up a 20 million dollar credit line. With the corporation flush with cash that much would probably not be required but it is always better to have a good reserve of cash for any unanticipated or unforeseen expense.

When he awoke on Friday morning it was a sunny summer day and to pass some time away until his 2pm meeting with Yelena he went to the marketplace to purchase 4 tomato plants. He dug up a spot in his back yard where there was excellent east and south exposure and put them in adding a little compost and lime at the same time. It was one of his favorite pastimes when married to Magdalina. Going to the garden to pick your own vegetables for salads and sandwiches was very fulfilling. He always threw some cucumber seed under the hedges where a tiny stream ran and his bounty was both profuse and large. Combining the tomatoes and cucumbers with some vinegar and oil is a pure delight for a summertime treat. When he had finished his gardening he cleaned up and headed over to be with Yelena.

Yelena Confesses to Sergey and Shocks Vasily

When she opened the door he could not remember when she looked more sensual. With a red dress, stockings and shoes highlighting her red hair and flushed face he threw himself into her arms. No words were spoken by either for a full five minutes. It was as if they had not seen each other for many months instead of the eight days that had passed since their time together in the basement sewing room. She led him over to the sofa where they continued to exchange hugs and kisses with her hand gradually moving toward his groin and his to her vulva. Finally she spoke, even as their hands continued with massage like motions.

"Vasily I hope you will not be angry with me with what I am about to say but I told Sergey that I am hopelessly in love with you and I want to have your baby."

With those words his tongue was frozen and he could not speak. Knowing she had taken him by complete surprise she removed her hand from his groin and moved it to his cheeks and forehead in a soothing motion trying her best to calm his emotions.

"I could no longer keep my love for you to myself and felt I had no other choice but to tell Sergey about my hidden desires and thoughts. He was willing to go along with the type of love we were engaged in, like in the sewing room but for me I had to be completely honest with him."

"We have a 14 year marriage and two wonderful and talented children but at age 35 and never having an affair outside our marriage I was beginning to feel lonely and adrift until you came into my life. When Sergey told me of his mistress in Kenya and their unusual sexual practices I could no longer provide him the love and respect I had given for so long. Vasily, life is too short and if you love me as I love you we should find a way to be together for whatever time is left on this planet for both of us."

He could not believe what he was hearing from the woman he cared so much about. To tell her husband she wanted to have his baby seemed implausible. The fact that he would be here in a few hours when the three of them would dine and then he and Sergey would discuss a business expansion that affected so many people was inexplicable.

Finally, Vasily was able to speak, "How did Sergey react when you told him you wanted me to impregnate you?" She smiled wanting him to use the words, "to have his baby" rather than the less personal word impregnate.

"At first, he was concerned of the possible negative impact such an occurrence would have on Pavel and Nada, as well as being the CEO of the corporation that was so near and dear to you. When I explained to him, I had a plan to make it work for all concerned, rather than constantly arranging little sexual trysts such as what happened the two previous times here, he was willing to listen."

And now Vasily's curiosity was getting the best of him. "Could you capsulate your plan for me now?"

"Yes, when the baby arrives no one needs to know who the father is. You and Sergey have similar features so only the three of us will know our secret. Pavel and Nada will embrace their new sibling. For my plan to work, you will need to stay in the Yaroslavi area and become a consultant for the corporation. I will act as the messenger who will deliver the communiques between you and Sergey. This way I can go to your home on a regular basis with briefcase in hand without drawing suspicion. As time passes and the new branch in the Urals is well established you and I can re-locate there with our child at which time Sergey and I will separate with Nada and Pavel sharing time with both of us."

Again Vasily was speechless. He had always wanted children but his ex-wife wanted to pursue a career and there was no time for family life. But now at age 50 he wondered if he had the virility and potency to conceive. However, he loved Yelena, and if she was willing to go to this length to give him the happiness he had sought for so long he was willing to consider her plan.

"During this interim period I assume you will be providing the physical needs for both Sergey and I. Also, while you are in the ovulation period of your cycle I assume he will understand he will not be permitted to have vaginal intercourse with you."

"Yes, I will provide for both of you but when I am ovulating he will receive only oral or hand relief."

With that, she stood up and extended her hand to Vasily and led him to the master bedroom suite. She methodically removed her red dress and stockings and then asked him to remove her panties and bra. She went to her knees to unbuckle his trousers removing them and his underwear, then using her tongue, lips and mouth to get him ready. Getting up slowly and not wanting him to have a premature ejaculation she laid down on the sheet of the bed and asked him to enter her vagina first with his tongue and then his penis. By this time she was moving her torso in a rocking motion and within minutes his ejaculation was forceful and complete. He rolled over and went into a brief slumber before hearing her voice.

"I allowed you to take a 30 minute nap while I was taking my shower. I will go downstairs and begin to prepare our dinner. Sergey will be here in two hours so why don't you get your shower and then you can come down and we can engage in some touching while I am preparing our meal."

When he had cleaned up and descended the stairs she looked as fresh as when he had entered earlier. She told him she was cooking him Russian lasagna and homemade rye bread along with a Greek salad. They hugged and kissed while both giving each a playful touch on the groin and vulva. In one hour Sergey would arrive and he couldn't remember being in a more awkward situation but she was as cool as a cucumber.

She then reminded him they would need to engage in intercourse in the next couple days while in the ovulating period of her menstrual cycle.

"Keep close to home and pay attention to your e-mails and I will keep you informed when the timing is right."

When Vasily looked out the kitchen window he could see Sergey's car pulling into the driveway. Although Sergey had a full understanding of what had happened in his house and bedroom before his arrival he was his usual upbeat self, giving Yelena a hug and kiss and Vasily a gracious smile and meaningful handshake.

"Ah, I can smell the Russian lasagna and the freshly baked bread. No one can prepare this dish like my little lady and Vasily you are in for a real treat."

His "little lady" seemed to be enjoying it all as she removed both her bread and lasagna from her double oven. And Sergey was so right, it was a treat worthy of the praise they both heaped on Yelena. She was special in so many ways and at least for the foreseeable future they would be sharing both her cooking and love.

After dinner Vasily filled both of them in on the land purchase he had made in the Sverdlovsk Oblast. Sergey deserved all the credit for finding the parcel while still working for Gazprom. They agreed they should move as quickly as possible to set up a meeting with the Board of Directors. Many contracts would be up for bids in Sverdlovsk in the next few years and they both agreed they wanted to be up and running within a year.

Since Vasily had achieved a similar goal when he opened the Yaroslavi facility, this expansion should be easier since he had already alerted their contractors and Morgan Stanley of their intentions in advance. It was now near midnight when they decided to wrap things up for this evening. Sergey agreed to notify the board members on Monday when they had their usual meeting on Wednesday to allow adequate time for their presentation.

It all seemed so surreal. Vasily's plan to retire early and travel to places he had only read about were now on indefinite hold. What was happening in his life was beyond imagination. In a way, it was like a dream, because a woman that he loved more than life itself, was now in complete control of his future.

The next few days he would be meeting her in some undetermined place in an attempt to fertilize an egg in her reproductive canal. Or, maybe that one sperm cell had already penetrated the protective wall around the egg after their Friday afternoon experience.

But this was Saturday and after yesterday's and last night's events with Yelena and Sergey he wanted this day to relax and clear his mind. He spent the day and afternoon in his backyard reading papers and listening to his favorite music. Yelena had given him some of her left over Russian lasagna and bread and he used his little oven to warm everything up. To think that if her plan worked in a matter of time he would be enjoying her cooking for many years to come.

It was about 4pm when he decided to check his electronic mail. His first one really intrigued him.

"Dear Mr. Sokolov: My name is Svetlani Cheranova and your ex-wife, Magdalina Breshneva, is a good friend of mine. I am the business editor of the St. Petersburg Times. While having lunch with Magdalina, she told me one of the most amazing success stories I could ever remember, during the many years I have spent here as both correspondent and editor. It was about a 43 year old man who had a secure and influential job with the government who gave it all up to start his own business.

In just 7 years he built a very profitable business with over 200 employees, and at age 50, he became a very wealthy man. He then displayed his generosity by transferring ownership of the Sokolov Cement and Concrete Corporation to his employees. It sounded like a fairy tale except coming from Magdalina I knew, if anything, she probably understated this man's achievement because she was a very conservative lady.

Of course you are the subject of my curiosity. Last week I told this story to our editorial board and immediately they asked me to contact you to see if we could do a short biography of your life which would run for 5 consecutive days in our business profile section. I know you will probably not receive this letter until next week since this is the weekend. If you decide to allow us the pleasure of doing this biographical profile

I will be more than happy to spend a few days in Yaroslavi without wasting too much of your time. Sincerely, Svetlani Cheranova."

Vasily had heard her name many times because she had broken many stories and exposes over the years and she had a sterling reputation for fairness, accuracy and integrity. It was not the kind of publicity he was eager to accept since his father was American and he was born out of wedlock. However, since she is a good friend of his former wife, he understood he would have to give her initiative serious consideration.

But this was the weekend and he would wait until next week to respond. A short time later he received this e-mail from Yelena.

"My Dearest Vasily, I will need to deliver an important communique to you tomorrow at 11am. I know you will understand its importance. Love, Yelena"

Of course he understood its importance knowing it would be another opportunity to implant his sperm into her fallopian tubes. It didn't seem like a very romantic way of putting it but in strictly medical terms it was an accurate way of describing it, since this was the path for the egg to move from the ovary to the uterus. For the next week he would have a crushing schedule. Probably, on Tuesday, they would have intercourse again before her ovulation cycle expired. Achieving an erection would be no problem since the very sight of her excited him.

Then, on Wednesday evening, he and Sergey would attend a meeting of the Board of Directors to present their proposal for expansion into the Sverdlovsk Oblast.

Sunday morning had arrived and Yelena would be here in a few hours with her "communique" and he wanted to do whatever he could to boost his sperm count so he prepared a breakfast consisting of figs, watermelon, hot chocolate and apple juice. Also, he had noticed yesterday while eating her left over Russian lasagna and Greek salad he had achieved a strong erection, without any thought of romance on his mind. After breakfast and his morning shower he was more than ready for her arrival, and good thing because when he looked out the front window she was walking up the sidewalk with briefcase in hand a full 20 minutes early.

After laying her briefcase on the entry table they were in full embrace as he slowly led her to his bedroom. She had this ritual about wanting him to remove her panties and bra while she removes his underwear. She tested the beds firmness by bouncing up and down while on her knees. She then requested he enter her vagina in the same way as Friday afternoon as she began to move her torso in the same rocking motion. They were both able to achieve an intense orgasm at which time they rolled over and took a short nap. She had never visited his home in the past, so he gave her a tour while both were still in the nude, giving each other gentle kisses as they proceeded from room to room.

"I really like your house but it needs a woman's touch in certain places and by that I mean I would like to spend more time here in the future."

"Yes, of course you have an open checkbook to make whatever changes you want. By the way, I am a very curious guy. How and where is Sergey spending his Sunday?"

"He went over to the company recreational facility to break in the new tennis court for a few games with a lady by the name of Darya Alfyorova who also works for Sokolov C&C. Do you know her?"

"Oh yes a very delightful and competent lady who heads the six person sales force. She is very athletic and I have seen her out on occasion running the hurdles. She has great form and I am certain Sergey will enjoy his time with her both on the tennis court and at the facility where her work ethic matches her athletic skills. She was one of my first hires and after four consecutive years being number one in total sales, I promoted her to her present position."

"Did you ever have a romantic interest in her?"

"No, no, she is a very independent woman and when I hired her had just been through a very traumatic situation with a minor league hockey hopeful whose ego exceeded his ability. When he failed to make the Locomotiv team he would go on these periods of immature behavior which she could no longer tolerate. She was 21 at the time and now at age 26 she made the equivalent of 2 million American dollars last year."

Knowing that the exchange rate was 25 rubles to the dollar last year Yelena did some quick arithmetic. "Are you telling me she made 50 million rubles last year alone?"

"Yes she had sales that amounted to fully 25% percent of our total volume of 200 million American dollars. We had a total profit last year of $20,000,000 and our profit on her sales came to $5,000,000. And this was after she was paid her full amount."

At this time they went back to the bedroom to get dressed but Yelena's interest in Darya Alfyorova and her compensation continued as they sat down in the kitchen to indulge in some cookies and tea.

"But Vasily, for a 26 year old female to have this kind of income which exceeds the average concrete truck drivers income by 40 times could generate a lot of resentment and jealousy."

"No, not at all, these drivers understand that for them to have a good job we need to have signed contracts and our sales force sometimes works around the clock to secure them. Out of our 200 million dollars in sales we designate 4% which amounts to 8 million dollars for our 6 member sales team."

"What is the gender makeup of the sales team?"

"Five ladies and one guy but before you think this is a little out of balance let me explain. Except for Darya all of them are university graduates who majored in mathematics. Trying to figure out how much concrete will be required for a 50 kilometer 6 lane highway requires a lot of skill and just a minor miscalculation can cost the company a lot of money."

"Surprisingly, when I advertised in the two major newspapers 80% of the respondents were females. I interviewed 15 applicants and the women seemed to be more enthusiastic and more forthcoming with answers to my questions. In the end my selections were wise because all five ladies outperformed my one guy the past five years."

"But Darya was not a university graduate. How was she able to circumvent the process?"

"She showed up one evening at the facility as I was closing the doors. She was well spoken, confident with an upbeat personality and a great attitude. She said she would be glad to start as a floor sweeper if necessary. I told her maybe we could find her a job as a clerk. We ended up going to dinner that evening and I was so impressed I decided to put her on my sales team. I knew she would succeed because of her competitive nature. She wanted to show the university grads she could outperform them and she did although they are all extremely valuable employees."

"With so many beautiful highly educated women in your company I am sure many of them would have been happy to satisfy your every desire. How were you able to resist Darya and the others?"

With that Vasily smiled, "I guess I was just too busy to notice. Besides, my patience paid off, because from the first moment I met you at the house where you now reside I knew I had to find a way to include you in my life."

She stood up and they embraced but before leaving she reminded him that she would be setting up another meeting with him on Tuesday afternoon at a place she would choose later. It was strange how their conversation had migrated to Darya Alfyorova because he actually considered her as a possible CEO to succeed himself. But he chose not to go in-house because there were at least four imminently qualified candidates and choosing one over the other would have created a very possible backlash. Although it was late Sunday afternoon he would try to get a head start on the busy week ahead by sending out a few e-mails. His first would be to Svetlani Cheranova.

"Dear Ms. Cheranova: Thank you very much for your interest in my former company. Currently I have been asked by the new CEO, Sergey Petrov to take on a responsibility regarding a sensitive issue I cannot divulge at this time. The issue should be resolved within a few weeks and I will contact you to discuss a time for a meeting convenient to both. Please tell Magdalina I send my love if you see her again before my next contact with her. Respectfully yours, Vasily Sokolov."

The following several days went by quickly with Vasily and Yelena meeting at the Romanov Forest Ecotel in their third attempt to begin a pregnancy during her ovulation cycle. And now they would wait for the estimated date for her period to begin.

Wednesday evening had now arrived and Sergey and Vasily would make their presentation to the Board of Directors regarding expansion into the Urals. After they presented their proposal, there seemed to be some reluctance by some members during the Q & A that followed. Their general thrust was why should they gamble on a new facility some 800 miles away, when things were going so well here? At this time, Vasily asked if he could address their concerns both from a personal and business point of view at which time he stood.

"At the request of Sergey I recently visited the site and was so impressed I wrote a check from my personal funds for 50% of the purchase price knowing it was a great investment no matter what the decision of the board would be. It is rich in all the resources and with a freight railroad running between the two oblasts we can ship those raw materials here at a huge cost savings. Also, we don't have to use any of our funds since Morgan Stanley is more than willing to lend the entire amount as they had done seven years ago when I started my business here. Now I want to say one final thing before taking any more questions. When I retired from the company my plans were to travel to the America's and beyond which I was looking forward to, but when Sergey asked me to go over to the Sverdlovsk area to look at this tract I was happy to assist him. Even though he is relatively new here we owe him a debt of gratitude. It's a win-win deal for everyone. I told him I was willing to give up my travel plans and move to Yekaterinburg and spend three years there to guide the new entity through the construction and start- up phase."

With that, Ivan Puchkina, who was the acting board chairman and a man that Vasily had considered as his replacement asked for a vote and it was unanimously in favor. The meeting was then adjourned with all shaking hands and agreeing that the corporation would derive great benefits from the expansion when all the pieces were in place. Vasily realized he had a real challenge ahead of him. He would have to re-locate to the Sverdlovsk area in the near future and this would mean either renting or purchasing a new home there.

But his biggest concern was how the move would affect his relationship with Yelena. With the possibility of her being pregnant and Nada and Pavel returning from summer camp next week he could only imagine the mental anguish she must be going through. But she was a very resilient and resourceful woman who seemed to thrive when she was presented with complex situations.

A Meeting with
Svetlani Cheranova

Since Yelena would be busy with her children the week of their return maybe it would be a good week to arrange a meeting with Svetlani Cheranova. He promised to contact her after resolving some issues with the company so he wrote her asking if she could visit sometime in the July1-5 time frame. Within an hour she responded.

"Dear Mr. Sokolov; Thank you very much for your response and offer. I have reserved a room at the St. George Hotel on Moscovsky Avenue for the 2nd, 3rd and 4th of July and arranged for a rental car. I realize you will have obligations during my stay so I will only need a few hours now and then to discuss the biographical profile of the Sokolov Cement and Concrete Corporation and the man who made it all possible. I will be looking forward to meeting you. Respectfully yours, Svetlani Cheranova."

Vasily then alerted Sergey and Darya she would probably want to spend a few hours with them in that time span at the facility and maybe a luncheon appointment. When Sergey told Yelena of Ms. Cheranova's upcoming visit she jumped at the opportunity to meet her and began to make plans for a July 3rd get-together at their home. This would actually be a great idea to meet the new CEO and his family since Nada and Pavel would return from summer camp by then. Yelena informed Vasily of her plans making sure he knew he was also invited.

As it turned out, having Ms. Cheranova in town those three days turned out to be pure delight. She went to the facility where Sergey gave her carte blanche access to interview anyone she wished. She was given the big wheel electric beach vehicle to patrol the grounds and went out in the concrete truck with a crew to witness a pour. She had a reputation for being thorough before putting anything into print and this was an excellent example in why she excelled.

The dinner party Yelena hosted the following day was impressive with servings of many varieties of Russian morsels. Nada and Pavel was back from Germany and when Nada expressed to Svetlani the desire to be a journalist one day she patiently explained all the pros and cons where ups and downs are commonplace.

But the biggest surprise of the day was when Svetlani broke the news that she had been a good friend of Bill Bond`s when she worked at a waterside restaurant in the USA many years ago. She did not mention whether there was any romantic connection between them. Of course Svetlani remembered vividly their night together at Chincoteague in her cabin when she invited him in with the words, "And Bill, if you get lonely tonight I will be here for you." That would be Svetlani`s secret today, just as Vasily and Yelena would keep their secret regarding her possible pregnancy and their future life together.

The time passed quickly and while driving to the airport for Svetlani`s flight back to St. Petersburg Vasily explained of the corporation plans to expand into the Urals and she promised to go there when it was up and running. It was a real pleasure to have met Svetlani, and learning she knew his father was completely unexpected, although surely she and Magdalina must have discussed this among themselves. With his father being so popular with the ladies (especially Russian women) he wondered whether their friendship had also extended to the bedroom. At least for now, she was not ready to make any confession.

The next week would be extremely busy for Vasily since he would have to fly to Sverdlovsk to meet with Ron Brown of Morgan Stanley who was flying directly to Yekaterinburg from New York. They would spend several days there to look over the property, and Ron would expedite the paperwork so the new entity could begin to access the funds required to begin the ordering process. Vasily arrived a day earlier to finalize the actual purchase of the land from Anatoly Asminov. He had used his personal funds to make the 50% down payment, and he would also use his personal money to pay the remaining amount, getting reimbursed later when Morgan Stanley transferred the loan remittances to Russian banks. Ron Brown and Anatoly Asminov were not only great to do business with but were the type of gentlemen you wanted to be among your closest and most trusted friends.

A Time of Great Joy

After bidding them both farewell he went back to his room at the Hyatt Regency and read this e-mail; "DEAR VASILY, I AM PREGNANT!!!." The implications were so enormous he realized his life would never be the same. Before he could begin to digest the news he wrote back. "MY DEAREST YELENA...YOU HAVE MADE ME THE HAPPIEST MAN ON THE PLANET."

He had always took pride in the fact he was able to organize his thoughts in such a way to attain the maximum positive results in whatever the task was before him. Yes, he was happy beyond his fondest imagination to have Yelena and their new baby in his life for whatever time he had remaining on this planet. But there were so many other considerations that would need to be addressed, such as how to tell Nada and Pavel they would be sharing time with Yelena and their new sibling, and their father Sergey living in different cities. Would they accept Vasily as their step-father once they learned he was the biological father of their new brother or sister?

But for now, there was no need to inform them who the father was until an appropriate time had passed after the birth. Yelena had always shielded her children from their father's affairs in Africa with his Kenyan mistress and she would continue to do so even after their separation.

Regardless of how this domestic situation was dealt with in the future, the reality was that he was committed to remaining in the Sverdlovsk Oblast for the next three years, to get this expansion of Sokolov C&C off the ground and running. Of course he would maintain his home in Yaroslavi and could fly there on occasion but he would need to rent or lease a home here for the next few years.

So today he would go out to look and lucky for him on the hotel bulletin board there was an advertisement posted there; "Executive Home Rentals and Leases." He immediately called the number listed and made an appointment to meet the agent at the site at 2 p.m this afternoon. When he arrived there, it was obvious some enterprising entrepreneur understood the housing needs of executives and their families, who had anywhere from one to ten year assignments in the area and built a community to fit their requirements. Besides a good selection of homes, anywhere from two to six bedrooms, there was a small office park, a child care center, as well as recreational facilities and retail stores within three kilometers of the community.

This is where he wanted to be and in less than a few hours he chose a six bedroom house with four baths in a cul-de-sac. Knowing that Nada and Pavel would be spending time here he wanted them to have plenty of space. It had a huge kitchen with all the modern conveniences and although it might not fit Yelena's requirements she could always bring Igor up from Yaroslavi to make any changes understanding they would have to get permission from their landlord. He called Yelena to describe the house and she was very happy saying she would free her schedule next week to come up to pick out the furniture.

The following several months went smoothly. Ron Brown from Morgan Stanley called to say all the loan funds were now in Russian banks and could be drawn upon immediately. Although Sergey and the corporation accountant were the only two who could disburse the funds, Vasily was granted permission to give verbal approval to all the sub-contractors, since he would be running the day to day operations for the next 3 years.

Yelena came up from Yaroslavi for a few days to pick out the furniture and they wasted little time breaking in the new bed in the master bedroom. He was able to secure adequate office space at the office park located within the community where they would reside. By the end of August all contracts regarding construction of the facility and clearing of the site had been consummated. The concrete hauling trucks were ordered and they would arrive in plenty of time prior to the formal opening now set for June of next year.

It was now time to interview prospective candidates for the three sales positions available so they could begin to bid on jobs. He called Sergey to see if there was a chance he could temporarily assign Darya Alfyorova here for about a month until he had completed the hiring and training process. Her job would be to help in the interviewing phase as well as help train the new recruits by bidding on actual contracts that would be let by the summer of next year. Darya was well suited for this task, and to think she was willing to start as a floor sweeper when she first came to the Yaroslavi facility one evening as he was closing for the day, to become the highest paid employee, is a testament to her hard work, diligence, and competitive spirit and attitude.

Sergey agreed Darya would be the perfect person to take on this important assignment but both agreed since it would be disruptive to her social life she should be the one to set the parameters. The next day Vasily received this e-mail from Darya;

"Dear Vasily; I am honored that you requested me to take on such an important assignment. I understand that choosing a competent and conscientious sales staff is crucial if the company is to have early success. I have only one request and that is that I could fly back to Yaroslavi for several days during my stay to attend to personal matters. I will be happy to pay for any expenses regarding travel from my personal funds. If we could get it accomplished in October before the winter season it would be best for me, Sincerely, Darya."

This made Vasily very happy but he insisted that her travel expenses would be paid out of the new funds made available from the Morgan Stanley loan. He gave her the choice of a small suite at the Hyatt Regency during her stay or sharing the new company rental house with him. Since the house was within walking distance of their office she chose the latter. He was certain Yelena would have no problem with this arrangement because their love for each other transcended any petty jealousy that might arise from less secure adults.

It was important to make as much progress as possible before the onset of winter so prior to Darya Alfyorova's arrival in about a month the sub-contractors were able to clear the site and pour all the footers for the main office and factory facility. With those two important functions now complete the steel envelope could now begin. The steel workers were a tough and hardy group and they could work right on through the winter. All through September Vasily spent as much as 12 hours a day at the site making sure there were no issues that would slow the progress they were making. He had learned a lot while serving as the general contractor and manager on his Yaroslavi facility some seven years earlier.

Today he would pick up Darya at the airport and decided this would be his day to welcome her but also discuss their schedule over the ensuing four weeks. When she arrived she was looking tan and fit. He gave her a hug and picked up a piece of her luggage as they walked toward the tram that would take them to his waiting van. "You look terrific so you must have made good use of the recreational facility during the summer."

"Yes, thank you I did, Sergey and I had some very competitive tennis matches. Also, I was able to get better acquainted with Yelena and what a special lady she is. Several evenings ago she invited me over for dinner and I was able to meet Pavel and Nada and I just fell in love with the entire family. Both children are so excited about the arrival of their new sibling in March."

As they drove toward the company rental house Vasily agreed they were all very special but he began to wonder whether Sergey might have revealed to Darya that the three month old embryo now developing in Yelena's womb was not from his DNA. Sergey, Yelena, and Vasily had vowed to keep it a secret among themselves until after the birth. They would eventually explain to Pavel and Nada who the father was and the new arrangements that would be required when Vasily became their stepfather. If Darya was aware of any of this she was not showing her hand because there was not the slightest hint on her part that she had any knowledge of their plan.

When they arrived at the house, Vasily gave Darya a quick tour of the property and she seemed pleased with the guest quarters. It was now 11 a.m and she wanted a few hours to rest and get used to her new surroundings and they agreed to go out for a late lunch at 3 p.m. After that, they would go over to visit the office where she would be conducting her first interview with one of the prospective sales candidates the next day at 10 a.m. Vasily had rented a van for her use during the time she would be here and it would be delivered to the office in the morning.

Having Darya here was a real joy. She was so upbeat and seemed to thrive on the challenge she was presented. As the days and weeks went by she worked relentlessly conducting interviews, visiting various government and private entities to pick up plans and specifications for upcoming projects, and by the middle of October she had hired the three sales people, all females, and they would go on the payroll on Dec. 1. In the mornings she and Vasily would make breakfast together and in the evenings when they were not going out to dinner they would combine their culinary talents to cook and bake some of their favorite Russian dishes and pastries.

She had taken only one three day break during her time here to travel back home to see friends and visit Sergey. Tomorrow would be her last day here and Vasily was really going to miss her. No matter how long of a day they had on the job they always took the hour between 9pm and 10 to have a drink together and discuss their day. They wanted to make their last evening together very special so they opened up a bottle of half century old wine and danced until midnight. In the morning, Vasily drove her to the airport and the signs of winter were now evident as the temperature got to zero on the Celsius scale and snow was beginning to accumulate on the highways. He waited at the airport until her plane lifted off and now he was all alone.

He was used to being by himself over the years after his ten year marriage to Magdalina ended but after meeting Yelena he craved the opportunity to be with her whether in bed or just being close to her. Darya was a most spectacular beautiful woman but during her month here there was not even a hint of the two sharing any time in the bedroom because it almost seemed like a father-daughter relationship. He was 50 and she was now 27 but from the day he first hired her at age 21 they decided on a hands-off approach.

Besides, only Yelena was on his mind in that way, and she would be here next month to spend a few weeks to make all the remaining preparations for the arrival of their baby in the middle of March. In Russia, the first two weeks in December was the beginning of the high season for skiing and Sergey had planned on taking Pavel and Nada to Switzerland to introduce them to the high altitudes. Up to now, there skiing adventures were on slopes under five thousand meters. Sergey told them their mother would go to Sverdlovsk to help Uncle Vasily with some of the paper work until his secretary arrived on the 15th of December.

November was a very productive month at the new facility. Sergey, through his previous contacts and employment at Gazprom, had arranged to have a natural gas line installed and was also able to have the sewer and water lines run through the same trench. Since the steel structure was now complete they could install the primary and backup gas generators and a dozen gas space heaters so the plumbers, electricians, and HVAC contractors could have a heated building to work in through the remainder of the winter.

When the 18 wheeler arrived to deliver huge bales of rubber for the roof it took just three days for the ten roof technicians to complete the job. At this time the project was ahead of schedule and under budget and with Yelena due here in less than two days Vasily was in a happy and buoyant mood. After another 12 hour day at the facility he went home and when he checked his e-mail he received this letter from Yelena.

An Accident, Grief, Despondency

"My Dearest Vasily…In less than 36 hours we will be together and I can`t properly express to you the anticipation I am feeling at this very moment. Before you came into my life I was lonely and listless without knowing what the future held for me. Now I am the happiest woman in the world. Yes, Sergey is a good man and a wonderful father and I have forgiven him for his indiscretions with his Kenyan paramour and the other lustful person who was a witness as they acted out their sexual fantasies on all those occasions when he was in Africa.

Sergey, Pavel and Nada flew to Zurich this morning for their two week skiing vacation and of all things Darya Alfyorova will join them after the first week. I had her over for dinner several times in November after she returned from her duty with you in Sverdlovsk. We all think she is the best and if I am not mistaken I believe Sergey and her have a romantic interest. I hope this is true because when you and I become wife and husband in the spring of next year I want Sergey and the children to have someone they all love and respect.

I rub my stomach every day thinking about our baby inside and to think in 4 months we will be able to hold her/him in our arms. I will be flying out of Yaroslavi on a YAK-42 airplane at 11am my time on Thursday which will be 1pm your time and since it is a two hour flight I should be at the airport there about 3pm your time. When I come through the portal to the welcoming area my heart will be pounding so I will probably throw down my luggage and jump into your arms.

I will call you on your cell when we takeoff. I know you don't like cell phones but on Thursday keep one close for me. Hearing your voice will be a reminder that we will be together in a few short hours. I love you more than life itself. Yelena"

He had not seen her since she came here several months back to pick out the furniture. Now that things were going well at the facility he could now free some of his time over the next several weeks to be with Yelena. Of course just the thought they would be sharing the same bed for two weeks was enough to keep his spirit sky high until she arrived.

He immediately sent back a letter expressing his love and the anticipation he was feeling as the hours for their reunion grew closer. When he went to bed his mind went back to the day he hired her husband, Sergey, to become the new CEO of the new employee owned corporation. Yes his business credentials were impeccable but when he revealed he had been married for 14 years with two children that was the real clincher. An individual with good family values was an important consideration.

At that time he had not met Yelena and little did he know at the time that their love for each other would transcend all other considerations. Through it all, the respect that Sergey and himself had for each other never waned. He understood after the revelation of his African affairs to Yelena she could never again provide him the satisfying love and respect one would expect for loving married couples.

The next morning Vasily would go to the office to greet the three new sales recruits. This would be their first day on the job and he wanted them to feel welcome and comfortable so after the introductions he took them to the local pancake house for breakfast. It didn't take long for Vasily to realize that Darya's instincts and expertise for judging people was a special gift because the three ladies she chose were impressive in every respect.

All three had outgoing personalities and their enthusiasm to get started was evident when they seemed anxious to get back to the office to begin working on the plans and specifications that Darya had left for them. Which one would eventually emerge as the leader was hard to predict this early but the one who had a special quiet charm was Lana Matviyenko who he later learned was a cousin of Darya.

Darya never mentioned this at the time she hired them but he was sure it was because she didn't want him to think she hired someone as a favor to her uncle. It was easy for Vasily to see from the start that Lana was a special talent and not to have hired her because she was a relative would have been a greater sin. After taking them back to the office he went over to the facility to be sure all was proceeding smoothly because in less than 24 hours Yelena would be boarding a plane in Yaroslavl for her two hour flight here and he was as nervous and anxious as he could ever remember. Yes he would always feel strange that it was Sergey's wife that had captured his heart. Yet, he was helpless to resist her overwhelming appeal as a human being, but also she had the ability to get you ready for romance with just a blink of the eye.

It was now Thursday morning and he wanted to be at the airport at least an hour early for her arrival at 3p.m local time. He checked his cell phone to be sure it was working properly. He very seldom used it because to him it was nothing more than a disruptive gadget whether you were having dinner or trying to engage in a business, or social activity. Electronic mail was his favorite way to communicate because you had the ability to choose the time and place to send your messages in an unhurried and thoughtful way. But today was different because Yelena would be calling him after getting airborne.

This December morning was sunny and cold. The local weather report showed by late evening a Siberian front of wind and snow moving in and people were warned to protect their pets and to purchase backup generators because power could be lost for as much as 48 hours. Since the storm was predicted to come in after 8 p.m, Vasily and Yelena would be in their comfortable home with its backup energy system. It was now about 10 a.m and Vasily went over to the facility to be sure all the people working there were aware of the pending weather event. Making sure everything was battened down and getting to their homes early to prepare for the upcoming storm was a top priority. He gave strict orders for all sub-contractors to leave the facility no later than 2 p.m.

While still there, Yelena called to say her flight would be delayed two hours for reasons unclear to her but nevertheless she would be landing at 5 p.m instead of the scheduled 3 p.m. There would still be ample time to get home before the storm hit but he was so anxious to see her the extra time waiting for her to be in his arms was a huge disappointment.

He stayed at the facility until all the workers had cleared out and as he was leaving Yelena called again saying her plane had taken off at which time Vasily decided to drive to the airport and just loaf around until she arrived. While driving over he and Yelena chatted about all the things they would do during her two weeks here. They discussed possible names for their baby which was due in less than four months with her selecting Jacob if it were a boy and him selecting Galina if it were a girl.

About 40 minutes into her flight the pilot announced he was encountering headwinds that would delay their landing and requested everyone turn off their devices and be certain their seat belts were tightened because it would a very bumpy ride the rest of the way.

"Oh Vasily I am so afraid but I will close my eyes for now and think only of you."

Vasily assured her that everything would be o.k. and he would be looking forward to seeing her soon. Whether she heard his reassuring words was uncertain because she no doubt heeded the pilot's demand and turned off her cell phone.

When he got to the airport he went straight to the weather desk and they confirmed all flights coming from the west would be delayed because the front was moving much quicker than their earlier predictions. As he looked out the window the skies looked ominous and the runways were already being coated with light snow.

It was now after 5 p.m and he went over to the Aeroflot desk and they confirmed that Flight 667 with 48 passengers was in a holding pattern and was waiting for its turn to land. By this time the runways were heavy with snow and the plows were out in force. Now all kinds of uncertain thoughts began to enter his mind. At 5:30pm he went back to the Aeroflot desk and reported they had lost all contact with Flight 667. He immediately went to the water closet because his stomach was in knots and the most nauseating feeling he had ever felt in his 50 years had overtaken him and within minutes he deposited his earlier breakfast into the toilet. At 6 p.m and then again at 7 still no contact with Flight 667 and now he realized that Yelena and their baby along with her fellow 47 passengers and crew had perished.

He lay down on one of the benches along with so many others waiting for their loved ones and finally at midnight Aeroflot announced that Flight #667 had crashed into a hillside about 40 kilometers east of the airport and all passengers and crew had presumably succumbed.

Everyone got up from their seats and makeshift beds and began to hug each other and the tears were profuse. His loss was beyond imagination and his grief was unbearable but now all he could think about was her two children Pavel and Nada. They were in Switzerland with Sergey and despite the early 1 a.m time he called Darya Alfyorova in Yaroslavi and when he broke the news they cried together and she agreed to contact Sergey and give him the news. Vasily knew she was to join them in Switzerland and Yelena had told him she thought that Darya and Sergey had a romantic interest in each other. If that were true then Darya would be the natural one to break the news to them.

When the storm subsided the next morning all friends and relatives were told that they were not to attempt to travel to the site where the aircraft went down since the only thing remaining was a small section of the fuselage. For the next several days Vasily was in a daze and he wondered if life was worth living. He called Sergey and they consoled each other both agreeing that Yelena was the most special of all the people that lived on this planet.

They agreed that keeping their secret was important for not only Pavel and Nada but for all concerned. Now that Yelena was deceased there was no good reason for them to know that she was carrying Vasily's baby in her womb and he would become their stepfather. Now he could remain Uncle Vasily as they chose to call him. Although there was no body to claim Sergey set Jan. 7th as a day of remembrance at the Assumption Cathedral in Yaroslavi.

A week had passed since Flight #667 plowed into the hillside and the remnants of the storm that night were still evident as the plows were still working to clear the highways that would eventually be cleared enough to get the investigators to within 10 kilometers of the crash site. They would need to hire local farmers with their heavy tractors to get their gear to the actual spot where the doomed aircraft with its 49 passengers and crew lost their lives. Yes the official number was 48 but to Vasily the number would always be 49.

For the remainder of December it was like being in purgatory. He remembered going to his office and to the facility at times but her final words consumed his every thought.

"Oh Vasily, I am so afraid but I will close my eyes for now and think only of you."

He would never know whether his words of comfort to her were ever heard. Since the accident, he was functioning by instinct only. He would need to think about returning to Yaroslavi to attend the memorial service to honor Yelena. He decided to declare a two week paid holiday for his office staff from the 25th of Dec. to Jan. 10th.

When Vasily arrived in Yaroslavi he called Sergey and he requested that he come over to the house to be with Pavel and Nada. When he entered there was a profusion of hugs and tears. Darya was there to provide the comfort and strength that was so important to the children at this time. In these days and hours of sorrow and confusion there is no substitute for the steady and calm demeanor of a woman and Darya was the perfect fit for the situation. This was the house where he first met Yelena and their love for each other became so intense and meaningful that both were helpless to apply the brakes although they understood the dislocation that would result for so many.

It was always going to be difficult to explain to Nada and Pavel how Uncle Vasily would suddenly become their stepfather but Yelena had a gift for explaining how real life situations change the lives of people many times for the good of all. Before leaving Darya led everyone in a short prayer and since the remembrance service was only a few days away Vasily and Darya agreed to meet there and sit together during the service.

A Day of Remembrance

This was a good idea since Darya didn`t want people to think she had any romantic interest in Sergey this close to Yelena`s death although in truth there was already an intimate relationship well underway between them which Yelena gave her blessings. Both women liked and respected each other and besides Yelena wanted Sergey to have someone in his life after she married Vasily.

The day for the remembrance service had arrived and the Assumption Cathedral was an imposing structure. The first church here was a wooden cathedral constructed in 1215 that eventually burned to the ground. The rebuilt structure was again destroyed in the 20th century by elements of the new Bolshevik government. The magnificent cathedral that stands here today was completed in 2010 and today it would honor the memory of a very special lady.

Before taking their seats Vasily and Darya were introduced to Yelena`s parents, Jacob Novokov and his wife Radinka by Sergey. Their faces and personalities exuded warmth and kindness and now Vasily understood why Yelena wanted their baby to be named Jacob if it were a boy. Vasily wondered if Yelena ever mentioned him to her parents, but if so, they showed no outward emotion because the hugs they gave to him and Darya were sincere. They seemed happy that Sergey and their grandchildren, Nada and Pavel would have someone to help deal with the sorrow and loneliness in the months that would follow.

The service would be led by a former classmate of Yelena`s with words that were so laudatory it was as if she wanted to canonize Yelena on this very day. She went on about how she excelled in every way.

"She was not only the smartest one among us but more importantly she was the most loved. She could have been successful in any endeavor she chose but her overwhelming wish was just to be a loving wife and mother."

Then she looked out at the pew where Sergey, Nada and Pavel were sitting.

"You must move on without her physical being but it is imperative that you keep her spirit alive. She would want all of you to look forward into the future. She was the most unselfish person on this planet and she would want you to pursue happiness wherever it leads so don't be afraid to move on. She would not only want it from all of us but she would expect it."

It was a very moving sermon and there was not a dry eye in the cathedral. Others who knew her from either school or someone who had been touched by her magnetism followed with short stories of how she had touched their lives in some positive way. As Vasily sat there listening he wondered if he could contain his emotions. Just like a woman, Darya, had brought a good supply of facial tissue to drench the tears.

Now it was time for the benediction and her mother Radinka requested that she be the one to do that part of the service since she knew her best. She immediately ordered everyone to stop shedding their tears because her daughter wanted people to be happy. She went on about all the funny things Yelena would do while growing up and now she had everyone in the cathedral smiling and if that was her purpose she had succeeded in a very robust way. Then she finished with this.

"At age 35 Yelena expressed to me the desire to have another baby. It must have been something to do with her move to Yaroslavi. She seemed so happy that Sergey was moving on to a new and exciting job. She didn't want to know the gender of her new one wanting to wait until the day of birth. As many of you know my daughter made all of Nada and Pavel's clothes and she began to make little outfits for both a boy and a girl. Maybe Nada will want to save them for some future time."

By this time the remainder of the service was just a blur for Vasily. Yelena had never mentioned to him that she was already making clothes for the future Jacob or Galina but it gave him a feeling of comfort that someday Nada might use them for her newborn. After the service most of the guests were gathering around Sergey and family to express their regrets, so Vasily and Darya went out quietly not wanting to interfere with other expressions of love since they would be with them at a later time.

Later that day, while home alone, Vasily could think only of Yelena and the mark she had made on so many others. When he fell in love with her the very first day they met, he knew she was a most special woman, but after today it was almost as if she had been deified. During his introduction to her mum and pap Jacob and Radinka they invited him to visit them in their home in Kostroma. They had recently moved there to be closer to Nada and Pavel. Radinka mentioned in her benediction that Yelena wanted to have a baby and she connected that desire to her move to Yaroslavi. He still wondered whether Yelena might have told her mother the identity of the baby's father. Up to now he believed only he and Sergey shared that secret.

While in Yaroslavi he went over to the facility to say hello to his many friends there. They were his employees just a short time ago but the respect they had for each other while he was their employer was enduring. Tomorrow he would have to return to Sverdlovsk so he went over to Sergey's to say goodbye and give hugs to Pavel and Nada.

As he boarded the plane for his flight, there was a light snow in the air and all his thoughts were of Yelena. It was just over a month ago that she took her fateful flight from this same airport. If he had any reservations about flying today his emotional state was such that it just didn't matter anymore.

But when he began to look at the faces of his fellow passengers he understood just how selfish he was. They all had families that were waiting at the Koltsovo Airport just as he and all the others were waiting that night. No one should have to endure the pain, anguish and helplessness he felt when all hope was lost. If someone feels as if they can no longer live with the gravity of their losses maybe they should retire to their favorite place, with a bottle of vodka, and enough medicine to get the job done without the loss of life for so many. But today, it would be a happy time for all of those who were waiting as their landing was accomplished with precision and skill. Vasily drove to his home on the cul-de-sac and tomorrow he would reopen his office and go to the facility to check on the progress.

For the remainder of January and February he did everything possible to keep his spirit alive and keep his depression hidden so he would not have an adverse effect on his fellow employees. After all, he had promised the board of directors that he would not only get the project off the ground and through the start-up phase, but to remain here for up to three years until the new facility was fully operational and profitable.

A Reunion on a
Sverdlovsk Hillside

Meanwhile, Vasily learned that the safety board had managed to clear a path to gain access to the hillside where Flight #667 had crashed, clearing what little debris that remained. So he began to plan a trip to the site where he could at least share her spirit. He knew the road to the vicinity of the steep hillside would only take him so far, so he would need a back pack, shoes for walking and climbing, and a few necessities. When he arrived in the vicinity he parked at a clearing where the authorities had prepared before taking whatever mode of transportation for the remaining seven kilometers.

About one kilometer into his hike he was approached by a local farmer on a small Soviet style tractor, "I can take you within 100 meters of the crash site. It will be slow but it will be quicker than walking and you will need the extra energy to get up that hill which is too steep for my "little baby." (Using that vernacular to describe his tractor) I assume that is where you are going. A few others were here the other day to pay their respect to those that were lost that night."

Needless to say, Vasily accepted his offer but what the farmer told him on the way almost sounded like folklore except he knew this man was sincere and adamant in his belief. He told of another plane crash that occurred on this same hillside some six decades earlier taking the lives of 27 skiers returning from Switzerland. His mother, who had certain spiritual connections with the other side claimed to have witnessed skiers using that same hillside on the anniversary of that crash each year until her passing.

When they arrived at the place where his tractor could no longer traverse Vasily got his back pack and began the climb. It was a misty morning and visibility was poor but he was able to find the indentation where the crash occurred. He took off his back pack and sat down and almost immediately he felt her spirit. He was not a man of religion but he closed his eyes and began a prayer and then he heard her voice which was distinctive and clear, "Vasily, Vasily, I have brought our new baby Jacob for you to see. Please open your eyes." And when he looked she was standing there with a sparkle in her eye holding him. "He is so beautiful Vasily, having your nose, eyes, and mouth. We are so lucky and I am so extremely happy, are you?"

Vasily was speechless. Had he moved from the world he knew just a few minutes before into some new realm where he would be sharing his life with her and their new baby? He was praying this would be so but when he stood up to hug her and hold Jacob she was no longer there. Had he fallen asleep for a few minutes and was this just a dream? No, this was real and no one would ever convince him that it was a mirage, an optical illusion, or that he had entered into some fantasy twilight zone.

His back pack was still there and now the morning fog was beginning to lift and when he looked down the hillside he could see the silhouette of the tractor and farmer. As Vasily began to move back down toward him he wanted to explain that his mother's revelations about the skiers was real, just as it was for him a half hour before. But as they rode back to his van he decided it was better not to explain what had happened preferring for him to continue to think that only his blessed mum was capable of having this out of world experience. When they got to his van they shook hands and Vasily handed him an envelope. "Planting season will be here in a few months and this will help you purchase the seed and maybe make a nice down payment on one of those new tractors." He protested that payment was not necessary but Vasily insisted telling him he would be back sometime in the future.

As Vasily drove away he began to think about the message that Yelena was trying to convey. Was she attempting to tell him the world she was in was so glorious that she wanted him to join her and Jacob soon, or was it simply a message of hope that his life was worth the effort, and he owed it to all those he cared so much about to soldier on? Whatever, as he pulled into the parking lot of his office his spirit was high and when he opened the door of his van the smell of cooked cabbage was evident.

It happened that one of the sales ladies by the name of Lana Matviyenko had made a pot of corn beef and cabbage the night before to celebrate St. Patrick's Day and brought in the remainder to share with her office mates. She explained her mother was part Irish and March 17th was an important day on her family calendar. Vasily remembered her from the time he took the three person sales staff to breakfast just a week before Yelena was to arrive. He was impressed with all of them but she stood out not only for her upbeat personality and good looks, but her eagerness and enthusiasm to take on a new challenge outside her life away from the university campus. As he remembered she was a cousin of Darya Alfyorova. And if this meal was a sample of her cooking she was way ahead of most 24 year old college graduates in the culinary skills.

For a moment Lana had taken his mind off his early morning epiphany, and when he got home that evening calmness came over him unlike anything he had ever experienced. Was Lana Matviyenko the person Yelena had chosen to help him get through his period of despondency? Of course no one could ever take Yelena's place in his heart and at age 50 and her being 24 any future romance would not be a viable option for either. Besides, she was probably married or at the very least in some kind of serious relationship and it was silly for him to even let the thought enter his mind.

But when she mentioned her mother was part Irish and March 17th was an important date in her family's life it struck a chord. Up to now, he had given very little thought to what month it was, let alone the day. Suddenly a thought hit him like a bucket of ice water in the face.

Yes it was March when their baby was due and when he thought back it was the middle of June during her ovulation period when they made every effort to begin a pregnancy. March 17th could be the very day of Jacob's birth. This day was indeed one to reflect upon and one he would never forget. Yelena and Jacob were as real to him as anyone he had met today and the fact that Lana Matviyenko had now entered his life in a way he could not yet understand or comprehend, gave him hope that he could rid his mind of all the demons that had taken over since Yelena's earthly demise.

Surprisingly, the next morning his energy level was higher than any time since Yelena's passing. He was anxious to get to the office to say hello to all the office people and then to the facility. The secretary and receptionist would be starting today but seeing Ms. Matviyenko was his top priority. But if she was to provide the answer for his "out of world" experience the day before she would need to take the initiative.

In fact, his best strategy would probably be to give more attention to the others especially the new hires. He was in high spirits when he entered the office complex and all those there seemed to sense his mood by greeting him with smiles, hugs and handshakes. He was doing his best not to make eye to eye contact with Ms. Matviyenko but when he approached her with his hand extended she threw caution to the wind and embraced him tightly.

Whether the others noticed her special gesture was doubtful since it was a part of her overall personality. But Vasily understood how meaningful it was because the exhilaration he felt was real. He was beginning to play mind games with himself; His time on the hillside with Yelena and Jacob; The farmer's story about his mother seeing skiers re-appear on that same hillside after it had taken the lives of all occupants some six decades earlier; And then, Ms. Matviyenko making him realize that March 17 was an important date to remember. All of this occurring on the same day seemed more than coincidental.

Each evening after his work at the office and the facility he would scour all the search engines to see if anyone had posted similar experiences. He was happy to find there were many postings but trying to separate the imagined from those of real conviction was a difficult task. He remembered reading a book titled, The Search for Bridey Murphy many years earlier and that too was an Irish experience.

In another case an intense love for an individual in your life seemed to be the necessary starting ingredient. A young woman told of a love for a deceased uncle that was so passionate that she contemplated suicide upon his passing. Then one evening, during her deepest despair, he appeared and asked for a dance, giving her a lecture on the importance of transferring the love she had for him to some other person who also was in need of love. Eventually, she found that person, and the happiness she had known prior to his passing returned. Was Vasily to transfer his love to someone else and did Yelena choose Lana Matviyenko to get him through his protracted period of grief?

As March turned into April and then into May the new facility was way ahead of schedule. The sales force had signed enough contracts for at least 16 months of work. So Vasily circled August 1 of this year for the grand opening. Between now and then he would attend the wedding of Olga Kornakova and Judge Jimmy Walker in Easton, Maryland, USA on June 17th.

He owed so much to both of them because his dual-citizenship enabled him to open a dialog with Morgan Stanley in New York and thereby obtain the loans for the original project and the new expansion.

Olga had sacrificed so much of her time in that effort and Judge Walker understanding the dilemma and embarrassment it could have caused her, sealed all the documents pertaining to the case. Vasily would never forget the time he and Olga spent together when she visited Russia for those two months in the summer almost eight years earlier. She was 40 at the time and now at 48, after losing her husband Ben Stevens in the terrorist attack in Pakistan, she would begin a new phase of her life. The next day he received this e-mail from Olga;

"Dear Vasily, I am so looking forward to seeing you again. I am so lucky to have found Judge Walker he is such a good and fine man. After Ben's passing I was so lonely. My daughters are attending school at Wellesley College near Boston. Marina is now a senior and Anastasia a freshman. I can't thank the CIA enough for setting up a special college fund for the children of those who lost their lives in the performance of their duties.

For now, I am still living in Easton and Judge Walker is living in Bethesda, Maryland. After our marriage I will be selling my house here and move in with him. It is such an interesting place with lots of fine restaurants. Our wedding will actually take place on the beach on Fenwick Island, Delaware, with our reception at Hannah's, just a stone's throw away. You may recall that is where I first met your father in the summer of 2010 when I was just 23. Although our wedding is on June 17th I hope you will come earlier because there is a place I want you to see. Judge Walker will be driving down to my house on the 16th so it would be nice if you could be in the area on the 14th. Sincerely, Olga"

Vasily had never told Olga about Yelena and it was better to keep it that way. Since things were going so well here with the new facility this would give him a chance to see a part of the USA outside his business trips to New York. He decided to make it a two week getaway so he penciled in June 10th to the 24th. After searching and finding maps of the eastern shore of Maryland he decided to make reservations at the Hyatt Regency in Cambridge, Maryland. He had the pleasure of spending some time at the Hyatt here in Yekaterinburg so it was an easy choice for him.

The town was just a few miles to the south of Easton so it would be a very convenient location. The hotel and spa was on the Choptank River which he remembered from reading a book by James Michener titled, Chesapeake. He called Sergey to tell him of his travel plans and asked if he, Darya, along with Pavel and Nada could spend some time here during his absence and he agreed. Since school would be out it would a good opportunity for him to get introduced to everybody at the new facility. Of course Darya spent a month here so she was familiar with the house and of course the three sales ladies since she had hired them. After all she was the cousin of Lana Matviyenko.

A dinner and a lot More

And speaking of Ms. Matviyenko, several times during the month of May there were packages left at his front door containing fudge and cookies without the name of the gift giver and he suspected it was her. Of course he could not ask at the office not wanting to embarrass anyone. Then one day he spotted a box of cookies and fudge on the desk of his secretary thinking that she must be the one who placed them at his home. If she was the one he couldn`t understand her motive since she was married to a man she seemed to adore. When Vasily walked into the office one morning Maria, the secretary, picked up the box and offered, "Lana brought these in yesterday and I am supposed to be handing them out."

Now there was little doubt in his mind that Lana was sending him a message. Had she developed a crush of some kind? If so, how should he handle it? Only he and Sergey knew of the arrangement between him and Yelena and they were the only two who had knowledge that the baby she was expecting belonged to him, not Sergey.

He began to wonder now if perhaps Sergey had hinted to Darya what the truth was and she in turn informed her cousin, Lana. He was hoping none of this was true. Yes, in time Yelena was to be his wife and she would be the one to break the news to everyone, including her two children Pavel and Nada. But Yelena had a special gift for explaining things that would make them understand that sometimes love is so overwhelming that it transcends all other considerations.

Vasily knew he would need to do everything possible to discourage Lana Matviyenko. For him, the memory of Yelena and their baby and the love he had for them was too strong to think of anyone else in a romantic way. Yes, he appreciated her upbeat spirit and she had become an important employee because her work ethic was more than outstanding. He could not afford to hurt her feelings and the emotions that would surely follow so he would need a road map that would consider all aspects of their friendship in a thoughtful but yet realistic way.

When he got home that evening he received a confirmation notice from the Hyatt Regency in Cambridge Md. USA that his suite and car rental would be available when he arrived on the 10th of June. He also got this invitation from Lana Matviyenko;

"Dear Vasily, I didn't want to approach you at work but on June 12th at the Opera House in Yekaterinburg there will be a special showing of Swans Lake at 6pm. I have secured two tickets and was hoping you could accompany me there. I am crossing my fingers hoping you will accept. Respectfully yours. Lana Matviyenko"

He had planned to tell his staff that he would be taking a two week vacation to America when he went to the office the next day and that Sergey and Darya would be here to look after things while he was gone. Since he would be away on June 12th he would have to disappoint her because it was probably something she had planned for a long time. He wrote back;

"Dear Lana, It was thoughtful of you to think of me as your companion for such a special event. Every time I go by the Opera House I am struck by the awesome beauty of the structure and swear to myself to visit there one day. Regretfully, I will have to decline your invitation because I will be in America on that day. Hopefully we will get the opportunity to attend on some future date but at that time I will extend the invitation. Sincerely yours, Vasily."

Adding the last paragraph to his letter would give her some assurance that there would be a future opportunity but at the same time he wanted her to know that he would be the one who would take the initiative. On the one hand, he didn't want to give her too much encouragement but on the other hand, she was someone who really lit up the room by just being there. In many ways she was so much like Yelena in that everyone who met her understood she was a very special human being. Like the woman he had read about earlier who had the OBE when her uncle whom she loved so much re-appeared after his passing to tell her "to find another person to transfer her love to" he again began to wonder if Yelena had sent Lana Matviyenko for the same purpose.

Of course it was her cousin Darya Alfyorova who hired Lana and Vasily could not help but wonder if she was the one who was having some input in Lana`s seemingly flirtatious behavior. Darya was the #1 producer at the Yaroslavi facility and Lana was showing signs that she too could emerge as the leader in the sales division here. In less than an hour after he had sent his last e-mail Lana responded;

"Dear Vasily, thank you for responding so quickly regarding my invitation. I didn`t know you were planning to visit America. I will look forward to your return and was very excited and happy when you mentioned that you would extend to me an invitation in the future. I understand that since this is the first day of June you will be very busy before your departure.

My two sales colleagues, Katya and Irina asked me if I could go down and take a look at a bridge job that presented some complications to see if my calculations regarding tons of concrete required agreed with their numbers. Darya taught us that anytime there is doubt we should adopt the system she had set up in Yaroslavi to double check the others numbers. The steel for the bridge is about complete and I was hoping you could drive down with me one evening to take a look before your trip. I think this will require your expertise and experience. Lana"

Vasily was confident that Lana could do the double check without him, but if she was intent on finding a way to share some time with him before his trip to America, maybe this was a good way to learn what her intentions were. He told her he would pick her up at the office at 3 p.m on June the 5th. He knew the location of the bridge project and figured it would be about a 50 minute drive each way.

The morning of June 5th was a sunny, warm Russian day. Since he would be visiting the office later that afternoon to meet with Lana he decided to drive to the facility first, since this was the day for some major raw material deliveries by train. They had installed a three mile rail spur from the main railroad line that would enable them to receive shipments of raw commodities from the mines in Siberia.

One of the lessons Vasily learned since being here was he could purchase sand, lime, and gravel there in 30 carload lots cheaper than he could mine them here in Sverdlovsk. Although the grand opening would not be until August 1 they would begin to fulfill their first contracts by no later than July 15th. In fact, the bridge project he and Lana would visit this afternoon would receive the first concrete from the new facility. When he saw the locomotive pushing in those 30 carloads for unloading he could think only of Sergey's wisdom and foresight to expand here and when Sergey arrived on the 10th he would be eye witness to the fulfillment of his vision. In both of their minds it would be a tribute to Yelena, the woman they cared so much about.

It was now 2 p.m and time to go home and take a shower and get into some comfortable summer clothes before meeting Lana. Although he was running a little late, his home and office were within a few minutes of the other so he was able to be there by 3 p.m. One cardinal rule Vasily expected from himself and others was to be on time.

When the time for their meeting arrived he had expected her to be wearing slacks, but instead she chose a one piece low cut summer pinkish dress and she looked stunning. Before he could get out of the company van she walked toward him with briefcase in hand giving him the kind of smile that most guys would interpret as an invitation for some future action. He leaned over to open the passenger door and when she got in she remarked how warm it was for this early in June. Her dress moved up to where her thighs were now in full view.

During the 50 minute drive down to the bridge project Vasily kept her busy answering questions about her family life while growing up and her time in college. She seemed anxious to talk about everything including the time she spent with her cousin Darya and how their fathers who were brothers spoiled both of them. In college, she dated several guys but none measured up to the high standard she expected.

Now her dress had worked itself up to where the panties that matched the color of her dress were fully visible.

Since Yelena's passing over six months ago, Vasily had no thought or desire to be with another woman in any way other than a structured social setting. But now, for the first time he was feeling the need to be with a woman in some intimate way. If Lana's goal was to get him interested for a romantic interlude before the evening was over he would find it difficult to resist. But now was not the time because they were pulling up to the job site and the steel workers were here.

When they got out Lana took the plans and specifications out of her briefcase and laid them on a makeshift table the workers used to play cards during their lunch break. When she began to explain that the plans she was given did not match the actual steel structure that was now almost complete. This really piqued Vasily's interest since at one time he was the Head of the Road and Bridge Department in Yaroslavi. Also since he was a graduate of Moscow State University School of Civil Engineering where drawing up plans for bridge projects was one of his favorite undertakings he was able to recognize almost immediately the disconnect.

Lana took out her tape measuring device and within a half hour they were able to uncover the blunder. Either the job manager or someone above him had actually increased both the length and width of the bridge by almost a meter. This would require much more concrete over what Katya and Irina had calculated from the plans they were given.

Whoever was responsible for this malfeasance would be dealt with in the appropriate way in time but for now, he was thankful that his three lady sales force was alert enough to recognize the mistake prior to the first concrete pour. This had happened several times at the Yaroslavi facility and the simple solution was to change from a contract job to a time and material contract. Vasily assured Lana he would take care of the details prior to his departure to America.

On their drive back Vasily suggested they stop at one of his favorite restaurants to have dinner. "No, I want to stop at the market and pick up some fish and bread and I will make our dinner this evening at your house. I have never been there and always wanted to see how you arranged the furniture."

He understood the implications well and it was what might occur after dinner that would give him reason for concern and yet he was looking forward to her subsequent moves and suggestions. There was little doubt she had complete control of the situation and when they left the market she let him know that she wanted to perform a dance routine for him after their meal. When they entered the house she took the groceries right to the kitchen and she marveled at both its size and all the modern devices that made cooking a meal a delight. Of course he could not let her know that this was to be Yelena's kitchen and she would become his wife.

Lana had selected a five lb cat fish but before she began her carving she asked him if he would mind if she removed her dress and wear one of the aprons over her underwear. Vasily understood well where this would eventually lead but he was now under her spell and there was no way he could or wanted to resist her requests and offerings. He had convinced himself that Yelena had sent her to him. Before she began to prepare the meal she asked him to come to the kitchen and when she loosened her bra she asked him to spend some time caressing her breasts. After a few minutes she went to her knees and unbuckled his trousers and when she had finished she looked up to him with these words;

"Vasily, I could sense you needed this kind of relief. Now I will make our dinner. Later, I would like to have a tour of your home and then I will dance for you. After that, I am available for anything you wish. I want to stay with you until morning."

Lana's boldness took him by complete surprise. When he first met her he was impressed by her quiet charm. But at 24 years of age and living on a college campus all that time, nudity and semi-nudity is no doubt commonplace. The home was equipped with an intercom speaker system and when Yelena was here last fall they had purchased some music albums so while Lana was preparing the fish and bread he put on an album by Rolf Lovland. He remembered Yelena's favorite from that album was "Song from a Secret Garden." Watching Lana in the kitchen in her underwear and apron and listening to the music created a very sensual ambiance and although she had completely drained every ounce of energy from his body a few minutes earlier he was ready for whatever was to follow.

The aroma from the kitchen would make any hungry man drool and when she rang the kitchen bell and yelled "come and get it" he assumed she was referring to the food. Before sitting down to enjoy the feast she had prepared she asked him to caress her breasts again for a few more minutes. There was little doubt this was something she really enjoyed. After performing that very enjoyable duty they sat down at which time she read a little prayer from a book Yelena had placed in the kitchen.

The meal she prepared was delicious beyond description. No wonder she declined his offer to go to one of his favorite restaurants. Of course, preparing a meal was only part of her strategy because what he had already sampled before the meal was some unexpected pleasure he was badly in need of. There was little remaining of the cat fish and loaf of bread when they had finished. He poured two glasses of wine and kissed her on the lips and forehead thanking her for everything. Then she wanted to talk; "Vasily, I don't want you to think less of me for being so aggressive from the time I got in your van this afternoon until now and what might follow later. Normally I am very conservative and cautious in my relationship with men and I was a virgin until age 19. I sensed that you had been through a very traumatic experience at some earlier time and you were reluctant to enter into any meaningful relationship. You needed a woman's love and I was afraid if I didn't act someone else would. After all, both Katya and Irina are beautiful single women two years younger than I and there was little doubt they had developed a crush too. I know I am selfish for acting this way but I hope by morning you will accept me for who I am and we will have other times together when you return from America. And now I want to dance for you prior to our house tour."

She had discarded her apron and still in just her pink panties and bra she went to the CD player and put on some music and then she began her dance. It was some combination of belly dancing and striptease and there was little doubt if this was her creation it was designed to seduce. She moved toward him and slowly removed her bra pushing her breasts on to his lips, then moving away giving him a most seductive smile. She again moved toward him, this time removing her panties and pressing her vulva onto his lips. And when her dance was over she took his hand, "And now I want you to give me a guided tour of your home."

As they moved from floor to floor she observed that every room they were in seemed to have the touch of a woman's artistry. The paintings were chosen by Yelena when she was here last fall selecting the furniture and there was little doubt she favored the mythical Greek gods and goddesses in all their nudity. He remembered the wallpaper Yelena had chosen at her new home in Yaroslavi when he first met her, and their subsequent time on the makeshift bed she had prepared as the mythical figures looked down seeming to approve of what they were witnessing.

Lana had never met Yelena and only Sergey and he were aware of the future arrangement that would eventually evolve had Yelena not been suddenly taken from them. He tried to diffuse the matter by telling her that her cousin Darya Alfyorova was here for the entire month of November while she was putting together the office staff and sales team. It was obvious she was having a difficult time digesting the news.

"Vasily, my cousin is a very beautiful woman, are you saying she stayed here all the nights she was in Sverdlovsk?" Vasily just smiled knowing what she was thinking but he explained from the evening he hired Darya as he was closing the Yaroslavi facility for the day it was always like a father and daughter thing. He wasn't about to divulge to Lana that he was deeply in love with Yelena at the time of Darya's visit here and was expecting Yelena's arrival on the first of December. In fact, both Yelena and Sergey were aware she would be staying here and both gave their approval for Darya's visit.

It was getting late and they both needed to get an early start in the morning so they took a shower together and when they went to bed she provided Vasily all the pleasures a man could ever want or desire. The next morning she made some poached eggs, toast, and potatoes as well as coffee and apple juice. After which, she put on her pink summer dress and since the office was just a ten minute walk and her car was still in the company parking lot they walked to the front door together.

"Vasily, I fell in love with you within a week after I met you. I wanted you to know everything about me. I understand it is not lady-like to move about in your kitchen in underwear but that was my fantasy and I was intent on fulfilling it with the man who was in my dreams. Last night you satisfied my every desire and I hope you got enjoyment in what I did for you. I want our relationship to continue on whatever terms you set. I understand you are still in recovery mode from some previous relationship. I realize I can`t take the place of someone that obviously meant so much to you but if you give me a chance and give me some time I will do everything I can to make you happy."

With that, he hugged her tightly and whispered, "Lana, I can`t wait until I return from America. I am so happy you came into my life. You have given me so much, and more than anything, you have given me hope that I can look forward to the future."

And as Lana walked toward the office the joy and peace Vasily felt was more than he believed was possible. Yelena was 35 and she is 24 and although there were obvious differences in the way they looked at life there were many similarities. Yelena only wanted to be a housekeeper and mother while Lana was pursuing a career. When Yelena was about her age she was already taking care of one young child with another on the way. He could only wonder if Lana had given any thought regarding having children of her own.

For the next several days he took care of any loose ends that required his attention including the bridge contract fiasco. Tomorrow, he would go to the airport for his flight to America and while at the airport he would greet Sergey, Darya, Pavel and Nada who would be arriving on an earlier flight from Yaroslavi. They would get to spend an hour together at the terminal café to discuss any impending business that would require Sergey`s attention during his two week visit to America.

The next day Vasily met them at the in-flight welcoming area and when Pavel and Nada spotted him they ran into his arms expressing how much they missed their Uncle Vasily and he made it known to them how much they meant to him. Of course, neither of them was aware, that Vasily would have been the biological father of their future sibling. Both he and Sergey thought it best to keep it from them at least until they became more mature. Vasily mentioned to Darya how valuable her cousin Lana was to the new facility without even hinting what had occurred a few nights before, at the company home. The smell of baked cat fish had lingered for a day or so but when he left this morning he doused the air with the sweet scent of roses.

Six and a half months had passed since Yelena had perished and he wondered how far Sergey and Darya were in their relationship. Yelena had given her tacit approval and blessings to their companionship not wanting Sergey to be alone when she married Vasily. In fact, both Yelena and Darya liked and respected each other and if Darya and Sergey were to marry before a year had passed, Yelena would have been happy for both of them.

Vasily Travels to the USA and Visits Olga

It was now time for Vasily to board a plane that would take him to London, and then to Baltimore with a connecting commuter flight to Salisbury, Md. From there, he would get a taxi to his suite at the Hyatt Regency Spa and Retreat in Cambridge, Md. He had studied the eastern shore map carefully both prior to his visit and while on his flights over. From Easton, where Olga was living, Cambridge, Salisbury, and Ocean City were strung out along Rt. 50 which covered about 65 miles. The distance from Olga's home in Easton to where he would be domiciled during his stay was about 20 miles.

During his flights over to America Vasily's mind shifted between his new relationship with Lana and Olga Kornakova. He would always be grateful to Olga and her prospective husband Judge Jimmy Walker for helping him obtain his dual citizenship. He felt a little guilty for the brief intimate relationship he and Olga were involved in while she was visiting Russia eight years earlier while married to Ben Stevens. And then Ben's sad demise while attempting to foil an attempt to bomb the American Embassy in Islamabad along with several of his CIA operatives. And now, several years after his passing, Olga would marry again.

The long flights over also gave him time to reflect on his life and his first 43 years was pretty normal. Growing up with his mother Galina and Vitali Sokolov in Russia he was content and happy with both his childhood and the formative teenage years. Vitali was a good provider and was able to fund his first two years at Moscow

State University. He did so well scholastically he was able to tap into government funds set up for high level engineering students who excelled in the field. At age 27, he married 21 year old medical student Magdalina Brezhneva. Their ten years together was respectful and fun at times, but never exciting except she loved the weekly massage he provided to her. Over that period of time she was the only woman in his life and he was pretty certain she did not have any intimacy outside their marriage.

And then at age 43 his mother Galina would give him the news that would change his life for the remainder of his time on the planet. He learned his father was an American by the name of Bill Bond. After that, he was able to meet so many wonderful people who knew him including Olga, Dasha, Polina, Svetlani, Arno, and many others. Indirectly, he met Sergey and his wife Yelena and children Pavel and Nada. His "out of body" experience when he visited the hillside where Yelena lost her life along with 48 other precious souls.

The start-up and successful venture that would become the Sokolov Cement and Concrete Corporation in Yaroslavi, and now the expansion of that firm into Sverdlovsk was something he could never imagine. And while there, Lana Matviyenko came into his life. His commuter plane was now landing in Salisbury, Md. USA but his mind was thinking of Lana back in Russia.

Vasily's taxi ride to the Hyatt Regency in Cambridge gave him a taste of the area. It was highly developed, but yet, there were fields of corn and soybeans that were beginning to mature into a harvest just a few months away. When he checked in it was easy to observe that this Hyatt was many steps above the average finer hotel. The word that would best describe its luxurious setting and services would be grandiose. The suite at the Hyatt he had previously reserved while in Yekaterinburg, Russia, was ornate, a décor more fitting to that area.

For the middle of June it was already 90 degrees F and he would need to find some lighter clothes. It was funny that a 35 year severe cooling phase of the planet had just ended five years earlier when many of the publications were predicting a prolonged mini-ice age with dire consequences. Now, some of these same media sources were already writing about global warming. We earthlings are so naïve and gullible.

Nevertheless, he had to deal with the heat that was here today and the week ahead. He decided to take his rented van and drive to Ocean City to check out their famous boardwalk and do a little shopping. He would wait several more days before contacting Olga. As he drove along Rt. 50 he stopped in West Ocean City where he was able to purchase the Bermuda shorts and light shirts he would need for his two week visit here. He had a custom fit suit of seersucker for the wedding on the 17th so at least that part of his wardrobe was taken care of while still in Russia.

Vasily's walk along the boardwalk was an adventure that everyone should savor. The smell of boardwalk fries, and the sounds emanating from the many arcades, created a festive atmosphere and for a total stranger, he felt like he was more than welcome here. In fact, he went into a shop to purchase tee shirts for Nada and Pavel and met a Russian girl from Tambov working there. They had a short conversation concerning their life in Russia and he informed her if she needed a job when she returned home he would certainly give her an opportunity.

The huge wide beach in Ocean City was peppered with sun worshippers, and the colorful display of beach umbrellas, could be seen for miles in both directions. He rented a chair and umbrella, and purchased some sun screen lotion, and now he became a part of a summer tradition that no doubt had a long history here. After a couple of hours on the beach he drove up coastal highway until he got to Fenwick Island and this would be where Olga and Judge Walker would be married in less than a week. For the next few days he would take advantage of all the amenities offered at the Hyatt Regency. He spent a lot of time on their two beaches and now he had developed a nice sun tan. Tomorrow would be the 14th so he would call Olga to tell her what he had been up to since his arrival. She insisted on picking him up in the morning for their day of leisure together. He remembered she had told him she had some special places she wanted him to see so he was anxious for the morning to arrive to not only see these places of interest but to see Olga again after so many years.

When Vasily awoke the following morning and stepped out on to his veranda it was already hot. He was happy he had purchased the light attire when he arrived allowing him to dress accordingly. She would be here at 9 a.m and the anxiety he was feeling made him both nervous and excited. When he first met her almost nine years ago she was just turning 40 and this year she would be 49. He went to the lobby 20 minutes early and within minutes she arrived. She was wearing light summer beach attire and there was no doubt the years that passed since he last saw her did not diminish her attractiveness one iota.

They embraced and neither wanted to let go. For Vasily, it was in appreciation for all her efforts in helping him obtain his dual citizenship and so much more. It was through Olga's tenacious effort on Vasily's behalf she met Judge Walker so they were both lucky to have found each other.

After shedding some tears together she led him to her black Lexus and they were on their way to whatever destination she had in mind. They talked about all that had transpired in the intervening years since she departed Russia in the summer of 2026 after her two month vacation there. She was reluctant to talk about her husband Ben's untimely death except to mention how the CIA had provided ample funds for the education of Marina and Anastasia.

A Spiritual Reunion with his Biological Father

As they made a left off Rt. 13 to 175 they were now in Virginia and as they passed Wallops Island top secret military installation she informed Vasily they were going to Chincoteague Island where his dad Bill Bond spent the last few years of his life. She mentioned that she and Bill had first come here on her days off in the summer of 2010 when she was 23.

"It was hard to believe it was nearly 25 years ago but I hope you don't mind if I don't mention too much about that summer since my days as a RIS agent are not pleasant memories. Your dad and I had a harrowing experience on the day of the 100 year storm where our very lives were in doubt. I will tell you only that through his heroic efforts we escaped the potential tragedy, after which, we had an intimate interlude at the Quality Inn that was located here during that summer.

I would rather talk about and show you some places we spent together after he returned from Russia in 2022. Ben and I were having serious marital problems during that period, when I learned Bill Bond had purchased a Cape Cod down here. Finding him again gave me a reason to persevere and go on. Yes, from that first day until his death in the spring of 2025, we spent many days and some nights together. Our relationship was both intimate and respectful. It has been 11 years since his passing and I still miss him today."

Needless to say, Vasily was speechless by her revelations. Yes, she alluded to some of this when she visited Russia during the summer of 2026 but never in such detail. For the remainder of the day she took him to all the places she and Bill frequented including the Cape Cod where so much love had taken place between them and now there was something she wanted to get off her chest.

"I want you to look at the window on the far left side. That was Bill's bedroom and there is where I got some of his DNA on my bra. It was kind of funny at the time because he had a pre-mature release before he could get to me. For some reason I decided to save that bra and you know the rest of the story."

For the remainder of the day Vasily and Olga walked the trails, spent time on the beach where she constructed a sand castle, had lunch at Cappy's Steak and Seafood Emporium, and ended the day on the hill where the venerable lighthouse was still standing proudly. She told him how they sat next to this landmark in his sand-mobile for over three hours in the summer of 2010 during the Great Storm.

And then, 15 years later she mixed his ashes with several containers of soil and dispersed them on that windy day in the spring of 2025. All day long she kept her composure but now she broke down throwing herself in Vasily's arms crying profusely. It was an emotional time for both of them as they walked down the hill together arm in arm and got into her black Lexus. The sun was setting in the west and indeed it had been quite a day.

When they got back to the Hyatt Regency in Cambridge they had a drink and sandwich and talked about their day and her impending wedding now just a few days away. She inquired as to why he was still a single man. Vasily had never mentioned his love for Yelena and their plans to marry or of Yelena's accident and now was not a good time.

"I suppose when you went back to America, after your summer in Russia, I always entertained the belief I might marry you one day. Of course, your decision to stay with Ben and make the marriage work was a wise one not only for both of you but for Marina and Anastasia. I have dated several women over that period of time and perhaps at age 52 it is not too late for me."

And then Olga in a kidding way, "In that case I will marry you on the 17th and Judge Walker can be our best man." As they walked to her car she mentioned that the same person who was the best man at her first wedding to Ben, in Kostroma, would do the honors again. "His name is Vadim Matei and he was a very good friend of your father. He is traveling all the way from Moldova to be here. Jimmy had given me the honor to name the best man, and he chose my daughters, Marina and Anastasia to be co-matrons of honor."

After their time in the cafe at the Hyatt Regency he walked her to her car and thanked her profusely for the time she had given him. Their day in Chincoteague would always be a memorable one for him. To think that both he and his father, Bill Bond, were fortunate enough to spend quality time with such a valiant woman was an honor and blessing.

When Vasily retired to his suite that evening he received this e-mail from Lana Matviyenko "Dear Vasily, All is going well here. I was happy to meet Sergey and his daughter and son Nada and Pavel. My cousin Darya seems to be helping them emotionally since the loss of their mother. I have heard so many wonderful things about Yelena. She must have been a saint. Although you had never mentioned her to me I suppose you knew her well. I really miss you very much and hope you will accept me the way I am. Since you have gone, I have buried myself with work and our sales force has ample contracts to last for several years. We started pouring concrete yesterday on the bridge project you and I visited. Thanks again for arranging a time and material set-up before you left. Vasily, you told me you would invite me to some future showing of Swan Lake at the Opera House. Just wanted to tell you they will have several 6 p.m shows on July 5th and 6th. I know you will be home on the 24th of June so you will have time to consider these dates upon your return. You mean everything to me and I will be looking forward to your return. With the greatest of love: Lana."

He sent a note back expressing his desire to go with her on either date and thanked her for what she had provided the evening they were together in his home. Of course what she provided was a great meal as well as the physical and mental relief he was so badly in need of since Yelena's passing.

But now he was in America and the wedding was just two days from now. He could not get out of his mind today's trip to Chincoteague with Olga. There was something about the island that was mystical and he wanted to go back in the morning alone to see if he could connect with his father in some spiritual way. He didn't expect the kind of OBE similar to the one on the hillside in Sverdlovsk but when he was near the lighthouse with Olga, where his father's ashes were dispersed, he had a strange feeling of complete calm, as if all the sorrow he had felt since losing Yelena had been lifted from him. He slept well and when he got in his rented van the next morning for the drive to Chincoteague he was rested and eager to go back to some of the places he and Olga visited the day before.

When Vasily got to the firehouse on Maddox Street they were having a mid-morning oyster roast and since he had foregone breakfast at the hotel this would be a great way to start the day. For a modest price, that would benefit the firehouse, there were at least a dozen varieties of oysters prepared by the ladies of the town. And it was a treat unlike any he had ever witnessed before. Yes, we have our Russian Table in Yaroslavi where many delectable morsels are served but this feast was all oysters and they were big and juicy.

They had arranged benches with folding chairs and Vasily did not hesitate to sit down across and next to some of the town folk and they immediately engaged him in conversation. He revealed to them that he was Russian and his father Bill Bond had lived here for several years prior to his passing.

"Oh yes, I remember him well and he was a popular guy around here. He was always willing to help in any cause and he was quite the lady's man too. I didn't know he had a Russian son. He lived in the Cape Cod on Loblolly Pine Lane and after he passed, Roland and Wilma Smith purchased the house from his estate about 10 to 12 years ago as I recall. I hear they will be putting it on the market and moving to Florida after the summer." Another gentleman who knew him also expressed similar sentiments about Bill Bond's generosity and community spirit saying he was always attending fundraisers for good causes.

As Vasily moved about the island he began to understand why his father loved its quaint and quiet enclaves, outside the hustle and bustle of the summer crowds and beach crazies, as they are called here. He went back to the lighthouse and this time he climbed the staircase inside this hallowed monument, and when he got to the top he looked over the landscape below. The serenity and peace he felt within could not be adequately expressed in words alone.

Somewhere below him Olga had scattered his father's ashes some 11 years earlier and now finally as he approached his 52nd birthday he felt their spiritual beings had finally connected. His day here had gone by quickly but he felt the need to go back over to Loblolly Pine Lane where he and Olga had been the day before to get another glimpse of the Cape Cod where his father lived for the last several years of his life.

When he arrived there, a sprightly lady wearing a wide brim straw hat was attending a magnificent display of begonia, impatiens, and pansies in the shade of several loblolly pines that adorned the northeast side of the property. His intention was just to have another look but when she flashed a friendly smile he decided to open his air conditioned van window and compliment her on the beautiful arrangement. Perhaps sensing he had more than a passing interest in the property she invited him over for a closer look.

She introduced herself as Wilma Smith and when Vasily told her his name, and that his father was the owner of the property before his passing in 2025, she dropped her water hose and insisted that he would need to come in the house and meet her husband Roland. After exchanging pleasantries it was obvious they liked each other.

They told Vasily they had never met Bill Bond having purchased the house and property from his estate. They went on to echo what everyone else had told him, in that, he was held in high esteem within the community. The furniture was included in the sale and Roland related that except for a change of bed wear everything was exactly as Bill Bond had left it when they moved in over ten years ago.

As they took him from room to room, he remembered what Olga had told him the day before, about making love with his father in the main bedroom where she got his DNA on her bra, which eventually became the evidence that gave Vasily his dual-citizenship. Of course,

Wilma and Roland did not need to know this, but Vasily did explain to them in some detail how and when he learned Bill Bond was his biological father. As the three of them sat in the great room Vasily explained to Roland and Wilma, that he had heard from people at the firehouse, that they were going to sell their house at the end of summer and move to Florida.

"Yes, when I retired 12 years earlier we were living in Baltimore. We came here to Chincoteague in the summers for many years and decided this was where we wanted to retire. But now, with me approaching 75 and Wilma 70 we decided the winters were too harsh and since we can't afford two homes we are going to sell this one and move to Cocoa Beach, Florida. I was stationed at Patrick Air Force Base when I was a young man and loved the area so now we will go there to spend our final years. But our hearts will always be right here in Chincoteague."

Vasily had become so fond of both of them in the short time he was with them and it prompted him to make this proposal; "I don't want you to think I am egotistical or vain but I must tell you I am a fairly wealthy man and want to purchase your home and property. The gentleman I talked to earlier at the oyster feast told me what your asking price was, and I accept, plus I will add a 30% premium. For the first five years after you move to Florida you can spend the summers here rent free if you wish. If you agree I can wire the funds to your account in the next few days."

They looked at each other in disbelief and Wilma wondered why he would offer such a generous premium when they thought they might have to come down a little in price to make a deal. Vasily explained if they took his offer to spend the summers here they would need extra funds for travelling expenses.

"I want to give both of you an opportunity to think about my offer. I will be in America for another week. Tomorrow, I will attend a wedding for a dear friend on Fenwick Island, and with the reception that follows I will probably need a day or so to recuperate. I will leave you my e-mail and phone number. I am staying at the Hyatt Regency in Cambridge. If you decide to accept my offer I will have my agent,

Ron Brown of Morgan Stanley transfer the funds and paper work to your account (s) within three days of your acceptance."

They shook hands and there was little doubt they had gained a lot of respect for each other. As Vasily drove back to Cambridge he had a feeling of contentment. Since losing Yelena there was a spiritual void in his life and this would help in his recovery. Yes, maybe Yelena had sent Lana Matviyenko to deal with his loneliness and perhaps his physical needs, and he was very fond of Lana but purchasing the Cape Cod where his father lived and passed away gave him an investment in America, and now the dual-citizenship that Olga had worked so diligently to attain for him was complete.

Of course he would have to wait a few days to be certain Roland and Wilma Smith would accept his offer before he could inform Olga. He wondered what her reaction would be because he never hinted to her he had any interest or intention of purchasing the property. In fact, it wasn't until he went into the house and walked through its rooms, thinking of all that must have happened here that convinced him that this house, on this island, was part of him.

It was late when he got back to the Hyatt Regency and after a nightcap at the hotel bar and a hot shower he was asleep in minutes. When he awoke the next morning his thoughts shifted to Olga and Judge Walker's wedding. Although it wouldn't take place until 6:30pm this evening the weather was cooperating as the intense heat over the last week was moderating. After breakfast, he decided to take advantage of some of the hotel's amenities prior to his 5:00 p.m departure for Fenwick Island. After using the exercise equipment and swimming pool he went to one of their beaches with his sun tan lotion to take in some rays.

A Wedding at the Fenwick Island Beach

While lying on the beach at the Hyatt Regency he closed his eyes and was in deep thought about all that was transpiring in his life. He heard the sound of a low flying aircraft no doubt heading for the Salisbury Airport just a few miles away. And now, he could think only of Yelena, and her fateful flight that snowy December afternoon. He would never forget her last words, "Oh Vasily, I am so afraid, I will close my eyes and think only of you."

The tears had overtaken him and he was hoping those sharing the beach would not notice. He would need to regain his composure and clear his mind because in a few hours he would be on his way to the wedding.

The drive over to Fenwick Island was one of reflection and all that happened in his life since his mother Galina informed him that an American by the name of Bill Bond was his biological father. He was 43 at the time and now approaching his 52nd birthday so much had transpired over the intervening nine years. Without that knowledge he would not have met Olga, Svetlani, Polina, Dasha, Sergey Petrov and Sergey's wife Yelena, the woman he would always be in love with. There were many more and his life had been enriched immeasurably by all of them. Of course, without Olga, none of it would have been possible and within an hour she would marry Judge Walker.

As Vasily drove into the Fenwick Beach parking lot you could hear the gentle waves of the Atlantic Ocean just a few yards away. When he walked over the dune the wedding planners were putting their final touches on their handiwork and what a magnificent setting it was. With a long red carpet, stretched under a canopy of blue, leading to the podium it was a scene fitting for a Prince and his Princess. And why not? Olga was that special and although Vasily had not met Judge Walker he was sure he was a special gentleman. The ushers were already leading guests to their seats, as two female vocalists, one Russian and one American would alternate love songs from each part of their world. It was unlike a traditional church wedding since this was the second marriage for both. Olga`s parents would be unable to attend because of health issues and Judge Walker`s parents were deceased.

The minister had taken his place on the podium, and soon the wedding procession began, and what an impressive group they were with Olga`s two daughters leading the way as matrons of honor alongside best man Vadim Matei who came all the way from Moldova.

Olga and Judge Walker made a splendid couple and as the minister began his betrothal message he led off with a few short funny stories, relating how they got to know each other by attending PLS meetings; "Professionals who have lost their spouses." Olga`s incomparable beauty, and unexcelled charisma, made her a very popular woman among the members but Judge Walker moved quickly and won the prize.

It was such a joyful event and one thing that is unique about beach weddings, they go very quickly, and before long the throng had moved to Hannah`s just a mile away for the reception party. And what a venue it was, with its huge deck and bar extending out into the bay, as the band warmed everybody up, with some lively music from the past. Olga and Jimmy were the first out on the floor, to do their rendition "fox trot" while Olga's daughters, Marina and Anastasia, were kind enough to extend an invitation to Vasily. While dancing they told him how much they enjoyed attending school at Wellesley College near Boston. Both were among the most beautiful and impressive young women Vasily had ever met.

While Olga was giving turns to the various admirers on the dance floor, Vasily was able to sit down and talk to Judge Walker for a short time. He vowed to bring Olga to her native Russia, for a visit in the next year or so, at which time they would have more time to talk about their mutual topics of interest.

Before long, Olga came over to their table and announced; "Now is my time to dance with my very special friend from Russia" as she extended her hand to Vasily. During their dance she pointed to the table where she first met his father Bill Bond 25 years earlier. When Vasily informed her that he was about to purchase the Cape Cod in Chincoteague, where his father spent the last few years of his life, she almost feinted, managing to blurt out these words; "This is something we will need to discuss fully before you return to Russia." It was hard for Vasily to discern whether she approved or disapproved, but for sure, this was not the time or place to discuss the impending purchase in any detail.

As the evening was ending, Vasily promised he would send her an e-mail prior to his departure to Russia, explaining his reasons for wanting the property. He understood there would be little time to have a personal meeting with her since she and Jimmy would be leaving for Cancun the following day for a one week honeymoon vacation.

It was truly a grand wedding and celebration and when he got back to his suite at the Hyatt in Cambridge it was already 2 a.m. He did a quick check of his e-mails and was happy to see one from Roland and Wilma Smith, saying they were inclined to accept his offer, and asked if they could possibly meet for a short time before his departure for Russia.

He wanted to go back to Chincoteague for another visit anyway, so, as he crossed the bridge on to Maddox road the next day, he felt as if his life was undergoing a transformation he could no longer understand or comprehend. Yes, Russia would always be his home, but he had a feeling that this island of Chincoteague was a part of his very being. Perhaps the spirit of his biological father, Bill Bond, whose remains were dispersed on the hillside near the old lighthouse, was part of his very soul. His purchase of the Cape Cod would complete the bond between them he so urgently wanted.

As Vasily drove up the driveway on Loblolly Pine Road, Wilma and Roland were sitting on the front porch, and when he approached they hugged as if they were lifelong friends. Although there would be papers to sign today to make the transaction legal and binding, their trust in one another never wavered. As they put their signatures on the documents that would pass ownership to Vasily it was only fitting that the desk they used was that of Bill Bond. He remembered Olga telling him that in these very desk drawers, was where his father had kept the two pints of soil that were to be mixed with his remains. After the signings were complete, Vasily called Ron Brown at Morgan Stanley to have the funds sent to the Smith's account immediately, and Ron assured him they would be electronically transferred within the hour. They exchanged their final hugs, handshakes and goodbyes but before leaving the island Vasily went back to the lighthouse and climbed the hill once more to pay homage to his father.

The next several days went by quickly and his thoughts now turned to his return trip to Russia. Olga and Judge Walker would not be back from Cancun until after his departure for Russia. He decided to wait until he arrived there before sending Olga a letter explaining his reasons for purchasing the Cape Cod, in Chincoteague. His stay at the Hyatt Regency in Cambridge, Md. was most delightful and he spent much of his remaining time there making personal contact with so many of the staff, thanking them for making his time at their place so pleasant and comfortable.

Back to Russia
and Sverdlovsk

The day arrived for the drive to the Salisbury Airport where he would take the first leg to Baltimore, then to Moscow via Heathrow Airport in London. During his return flight, he thought of all the memorable times visiting and meeting so many wonderful people who became his personal friends in America. But now he would be returning to Sverdlovsk where he would resume his responsibilities at the new facility. Sergey Petrov and Darya Alfyorova who had taken his place while visiting America would return to Yaroslavi with Nada and Pavel. When his plane touched down at Domodedova in Moscow he got an e-mail from Sergey saying they would be returning to Yaroslavi today and had left the facility at Sverdlovsk in charge of Lana Matviyenko until he arrived.

He realized it was his way of telling Vasily that Ms. Matviyenko was quite capable of being a CEO one day, and maybe he should consider her as his replacement, when his commitment in Sverdlovsk was over. Vasily remembered that he had an appointment with Lana at the Opera House in a few weeks from now, but he missed her so much all he could think about was holding her in his arms again. He was still in a fog from his long flight and had lost track of day and time. After checking his watch it was Saturday, June 26th at 1pm. He went over to the information desk and learned he could get a local flight to Koltsova Airport in Yekaterinburg with a 2:55 departure time. He immediately called Lana and asked if she could pick him up upon arrival at the airport and spend the evening with him at home. Her voice gave him the answer he wanted to hear. "Oh Vasily, you just made me the happiest woman on the planet." It was a line she had used before but this time it had a very special meaning because his desire to be with her was overwhelming.

A few hours later, his plane touched down at Koltsova and when he arrived at the welcoming area for incoming passengers she was easy to recognize. Wearing a light orange summer ensemble she was spectacular in every way. She was even more beautiful than he could remember and being twice her age their tight embrace must have created a stir among the crowd that had assembled. But Lana didn't allow their stares to stop her from displaying her emotion and affection, with tears of joy, as they walked through the airport hand in hand.

It had been several weeks since they were together in his home when she prepared a catfish dinner for him in her panties and bra. And now they were pulling in the driveway and the anticipation of what was to follow once inside was what every man dreams of. During the drive over she massaged his inner thighs with a slow circular motion touching his most sensitive places in a teasing way and she could sense he was more than ready. Once through the door Lana wasted little time, "I will prepare some night caps and see you upstairs in 20 minutes."

Vasily got a hot shower and entered the main bedroom where Lana had already placed the drinks on the night table wearing only her orange panties and bra. After a brief toast their bodies became one and all Vasily wanted was to hold her close while massaging her vulva and teasing her nipples with his tongue as she reciprocated in every way. By the time they went to sleep it must have been in the early morning hours because when he picked up his watch it was 10am on Sunday morning and she was no longer in his arms. The distinctive smell of pork scrapple was in the air and when he got to the kitchen she was standing over the stove with a sheer white negligee covering her now bright red panties and bra.

His trip to America was a memorable one but being back home in Russia with such a spectacular woman and human being was more than anyone could ask. After a kiss and embrace they sat down to a hearty breakfast of fruit, scrapple and Russian pancakes. Up to now, she had taken all the initiative to develop a relationship. Vasily realized he had not given his full appreciation to a woman who was not only a great lover but a special talent with a limitless potential to be a future CEO. He extended his right hand to hers and whispered, "Thanks so much for coming into my life." This was an emotional moment for her as tears formed in her eyes, "Vasily, you mean everything to me. I will be happy to be yours in any capacity you wish."

After breakfast they sat down to discuss all that had transpired at the facility since he was gone. She was effusive in her praise of Sergey Petrov and her cousin Darya Alfyorova as they worked as a team to keep the new facility on the path of progress Vasily had set prior to his trip to America. Lana expressed how fortunate she was to have met Sergey's two children, Nada and Pavel. "Their mother, Yelena, must have been so special because both of her children were the epitome of good manners with talents beyond their years. Russia is so fortunate to have young people like them in the pipeline so to speak. They will be our future leaders." Vasily agreed with her assessment but he could not help but think that Yelena carried his son, Jacob in her womb when both lost their lives that snowy, windy evening on the hillside just north of Koltsova. Only he and Sergey knew that the five month embryo she carried was his and it would be their secret.

After breakfast, they retired to the study, where Lana briefed Vasily of all the impending business and contracts that would require his attention over the next several weeks. She also reminded him of their Opera House engagement on July 5th and their official grand opening ceremony on August 1. It was now late Sunday evening when they retired to the bedroom and like the night before their naked bodies became one as they fell asleep in full appreciation of each other.

When Monday morning arrived Vasily got their breakfast together with some oatmeal, toast and fruit. He wanted to take the day off to send some e-mails to his friends in America. He asked Lana to take on his responsibilities for the day but would be ready for full duty by 7am Tuesday morning. Lana expressed that she would be honored to take on the challenge but would include the entire office staff as equal CEO's not wanting to think she was given some special consideration. Vasily agreed it was a good idea as they kissed and embraced one more time before she walked to the office, just a few minutes away.

Olga and Judge Walker would be returning to their Maryland home today from their one week honeymoon vacation in Cancun. His first e-mail would be to Olga explaining his reasons for purchasing the Cape Cod his father once owned in Chincoteague. He told her he wanted to invest in America in some way, and during his short time on the island, he not only fell in love with its raw natural beauty, but it also provided a spiritual link that was missing from his life.

For the next several weeks Vasily got re-acquainted with his staff and visited every job site the company had contracts with. He wanted them to know that the Sokolov Corporation would provide not only their cement and concrete requirements, but also, any technical support they may need from their engineering department. While he was in America Sergey hired Dmitry Cherkin, an experienced engineer, with impeccable credentials to head the new office of civil engineering with the dual duty as outside supervisor. On many of his visits to the sites Dmitry would accompany him and Vasily could not have been more impressed. He was a very capable and competent engineer as well of possessing the kind of engaging personality, that could totally disarm even the most strident and difficult person within minutes. If a customer had a legitimate complaint Dmitry assured them he would personally address the matter until all parties were satisfied with the outcome.

Having Dmitry taking care of any issues on the job sites and Lana expanding her duties at the office gave him the confidence and freedom to make short visits to other venues to attend to both personal and business matters without the worry he had earlier trying to get the new entity up and running. Of course Lana continued to provide the companionship he so desperately needed after losing Yelena. Yes she was a great lover but having her accompany him for dinner and social events made life so much more tolerable. They attended the Opera to see Swan Lake and many other plays in the ensuing months as well as being the hosts for company picnics and parties as well as the one for the Grand Opening Party.

It was hard to believe that over two years had passed since Vasily arrived in Sverdlovsk to undertake the responsibility for the new expansion of the Sokolov Cement and Concrete Corporation. They were meeting all their financial responsibilities with on time payments and when Vasily and the comptroller from the Yaroslavi office went over the books they projected within a year the new entity would be in the black. That would coincide with the final year of his commitment here in Sverdlovsk and he would then be free to travel or visit all the places he once dreamed of prior to meeting Yelena and taking on the job here.

But now he had to think of his relationship with Lana Matviyenko. She had hinted at marriage but the difference in ages between them it seemed unfair to burden her when she had such a bright future ahead. Yes, she and Dmitry Cherkin would probably take over as CEO and Vice CEO with Sergey Petrov now becoming Chairman at both locations. Sergey would almost certainly ask the board to appoint Darya Alfyorova as Vice-Chair of both entities. Dmitry and Lana would report to them in the line of command. To have two women in such high position was out of the ordinary for a Russian corporation but both were very deserving and well qualified and the fact that Darya and Lana were cousins didn't matter in the least.

Time had passed quickly since Vasily returned from his visit to America and he received an e-mail from Roland and Wilma Smith saying they would accept his offer to spend the summer in Chincoteague at his Cape Cod. They loved their new home in Cocoa Beach, Florida but could not resist coming back to visit old friends and taking part in all the oyster and crab festivals. Also, they still loved the old house and property they purchased years earlier from the estate of Bill Bond. Vasily had taken the option of paying his real estate taxes for three years in advance prior to leaving America, and hired a caretaker to check his property at regular intervals to be sure all the systems were in good working order, as well as checking for any possible storm damage to the structure.

It was his piece of America although he didn't know when he would get to re-visit the Delmarva area that he had grown so fond of. Olga and Judge Walker were now living in Bethesda, Md. USA and were using the Easton home for a get-away venue, as well as a place where Marina and Anastasia could return for future visits to the area. Vasily wrote back to the Smith's saying how happy he was that they were taking advantage of his offer and hoped they would continue to come back in future summers.

Vasily still had some time remaining on his commitment at the Sverdlovsk facility but with Lana and Dmitry here he felt confident enough to take a week off to visit Yaroslavi where he still maintained the home he purchased when he first moved to Yaroslavi many years earlier when he took the job as Administrator of Roads and Bridges. Olga and Yelena had visited him there, where both had sat in the chair he inherited from his mother Galina. While in Yaroslavi, he would also have time to visit Sergey at the house the company purchased for him and Yelena when they first came to Yaroslavi to assume their new duties.

When Vasily arrived in Yaroslavi, after a short visit to his home he went over to see Sergey and family. He had a wonderful reunion with Sergey, Nada, and Pavel, as well as Darya Alfyorova, who was still providing the moral support both children needed since the loss of their mother Yelena. Darya chided Vasily about when he was going to ask her cousin Lana to marry him and Vasily shot back wondering when her and Sergey would be tying the knot. "Sooner than you think" she responded and this took Vasily by complete surprise.

There was little doubt this would be good for the children as well as Sergey but he decided not to ask about their future arrangements, allowing them to break the news at the appropriate time. It was right here at this very house when it contained no furniture that Vasily met Yelena for the first time. It was love from the very beginning and he would never forget all that had transpired here. Their time in the master bedroom suite in the makeshift bed before they moved in, and later in the basement sewing room while Sergey, Pavel and Nada were engaged in a game of chess on the floor above.

At the time Yelena knew that one day she would be leaving Sergey because she could no longer endure his propensity to experiment into what she considered deviant sexual practices. Vasily could not help but wonder how Darya was dealing with Sergey's sexual addiction. After all, they had been together for several years now and should be well aware of what she was dealing with by this time. Darya was a strong person and since they were both sports enthusiasts maybe he was burning up the extra energy with their tennis, swimming and running track around the oval at the recreation area.

Nevertheless, it wasn't any of his business and if Darya could adapt to his vagaries, that is all that mattered, and the fact she hinted they would be husband and wife before long, provided ample proof that their feelings for each other transcended any concern she might have harbored.

While there, Vasily and Sergey talked about all the progress being made in Sverdlovsk and the possible leadership appointments after his departure next year. They both agreed on the names and positions that should be submitted to the board and although it was an employee owned corporation it was highly doubtful anyone would resist the recommendations of both Vasily and Sergey.

After a few days back in Yaroslavi visiting friends and employees at the old facility Vasily decided to drive to Kostroma to visit Jacob and Radinka Novokov, the parents of Yelena. He didn't know them well but at the requiem services for Yelena at the cathedral several years ago they invited him to visit them some day in the future. As far as Vasily knew, only he and Sergey knew the identity of the father of their future grandchild. Radinka had mentioned in her tribute to her daughter that Yelena she was looking forward to being a mother again at age 35. If the baby was a male she already had given the future boy the name of Jacob after her father.

Vasily's trip to Kostroma went by quickly and when he arrived at their home Radinka came to the door and to his surprise she recognized him and gave him a welcoming hug. "Please come in, it is so nice of you to visit especially at this time. I just returned from the hospital. My husband Jacob took ill two weeks ago and I have been told he has but a few more days before God will take him from me. Some viral lung condition that was lying dormant for many years and then suddenly sprung up almost overnight. He was a heavy smoker years ago and no doubt in those years the seeds were planted deciding just now to show their ugly head." Vasily was speechless as this was something he didn't expect and he wondered why Sergey didn't mention Mr. Novokov's condition a few days earlier when he visited his home. Then Radinka continued, "I decided not to tell Sergey because Nada and Pavel are in their final exams at school and Jacob implored me not to reveal his condition to them at this crucial time in their lives. Besides, he didn't want them to see him in his weakened condition, preferring them to remember him when he was in good health playing chess and visiting the parks and museums with them. I am sorry to give you this news because I know you are a busy man and must have intended to stop by for just a short time on your way to an important meeting."

With this, Vasily assured her that his only reason for driving to Kostroma was to visit them. "In that case you have made me very happy because there is much I want to discuss with you. Come back to the parlor and I will prepare a cool drink for both of us. I know after the long drive your throat must be dry."

As he sat there in the chair waiting for her to bring the drinks he understood exactly what the conversation would be about. She was such a pleasant woman and even in her moment of grief her face projected a calm and ease that reminded him of Yelena as she sat the glass of apple cider in front of him and took the chair opposite the small eighteenth century table.

"You see Mr. Sokolov, I am a woman of faith and I can't tell you how many times I wanted to write to you to express my thanks for making my daughter such a happy person. Yes, she told me that you were the father of our future grandson Jacob. At some point everyone would learn this, but she asked me to keep it a secret until sometime in the future. I didn't even tell my husband Jacob."

At this point Vasily could not speak a word but yet, he felt a giant burden had been lifted from his mind. And then Radinka continued, "Yelena told me that after about 12 years in her marriage with Sergey there were certain things that occurred between them that made it impossible for a reconciliation of their differences. She did not describe to me the circumstances of her unhappiness. This was all before she moved to Yaroslavi and I am sure some months before she met you. During that period she was listless and lethargic. After her very first visit to the house in Yaroslavi she became a different daughter and person. She came out of her doldrums and told me she was looking forward to their move. Some months after their move she told me the entire story about the man she met, who had given her the happiness she was so desperately in need of, and that she would bear his child."

With this, Vasily broke into a tearful sob that he could not subdue. She walked over and hugged him and after a few minutes he was able to explain how he fell in love with her daughter almost from the very first minute.

"When she got out of her car at the parking space of her new home she had a charisma and charm in the way she walked, the way she smiled, and the way she spoke. I understood she was the wife of the man I had just hired to be the CEO of the corporation I started. In the span of seven years the company was very successful and I became wealthy but because it consumed every minute of my time I was tired and was in need of a CEO to take over the day to day duties. I recruited Sergey and to this day I don't regret my decision. He is a knowledgeable and gifted leader and he has made the Sokolov Cement and Concrete Corporation a more vibrant and exciting company. Sergey encouraged the Board of Directors to expand into the Sverdlovsk area and I can personally attest that it was a wise decision. It is up and running in just two short years and when I leave there next year it will already be turning a healthy profit, but I have digressed. I never quite understood the problems Sergey and Yelena were having in their marriage. Their decision to eventually divorce was no doubt made prior to our meeting each other. They were probably delaying their separation until Pavel and

Nada got well established in their new school and new surroundings. After two years the children seems to have adjusted well and maybe one day both of them will work for the corporation. They are both brilliant kids and every company needs young people like them to inject new ideas and innovation so the business never gets stale."

In this short amount of time Radinka and Vasily had gained great respect for each other and when she informed Vasily the Bishop would be at the hospital at 7pm to give her husband the final sacraments and prayer Vasily asked if he could accompany her. She agreed it would be an uplifting moment for him and when the hour arrived they went together. When Radinka explained to Jacob who was here to visit he perked up almost immediately.

"My son-in-law and grandchildren would talk about you quite frequently and I must say it was almost in a reverent way. I met you at the cathedral for a short time during our daughter's service. When Sergey accepted the position with your company my daughter Yelena's life seemed to take on a new meaning. She told me many times what a wonderful person you were and you were the one who helped renew her spirit and vitality and I thank you very much."

Hearing this from a man who was so close to death was an emotional moment for Vasily and he took both his hands and raised Jacob's arm carefully while whispering in a most respectful way, "Sir, it is such an honor to be with you and Radinka today. Your daughter was the kindest and most special person I have ever known. And now I know why, because her parents exemplify what love is all about. Because of both of you she excelled in every way. No doubt you also had a very positive influence on Pavel and Nada because they will become our future in whatever field they choose to enter."

After they exchanged a few more thoughts the Bishop appeared and Vasily stepped out of the room so the three of them could be together at this solemn time. Later, as Radinka and Vasily drove back to her domicile she remarked that the Bishop told her that her husband's condition was not as dire as he thought just several days ago when he last visited. His spirit is high so instead of less than a few days he will probably be with us for a longer time. This news made Radinka very happy since every extra day she had him in her life was a blessing she would always cherish.

As Vasily drove back to Yaroslavi he felt the presence of Yelena. It was as if she was in the van with him. Being with the Novokovs for just this short visit is something he would never forget. He was happy that Yelena had told Radinka that the baby boy she was carrying in her womb belonged to him. She knew that her daughter would not have allowed this to happen without great thought and overwhelming love and respect for the man she spoke of in the most glowing terms.

When he arrived back home he sat in the chair that his mother Galina had passed on to him many years ago. He bowed his head and thanked the heavens for giving him the intestinal fortitude to visit the Novokovs. After all, if he had not entered Yelena's life she would be alive today. But they greeted him with the kind of love you would expect from a close member of the family. Like Yelena, they were exceptional in every way and just to be with them for a short amount of time today was an experience he would always savor.

Before retiring for the evening he fixed himself a gin and tonic and after taking a hot shower and checked his electronic mail and received this note from Lana. "My Dearest Vasily, I hope you are enjoying your stay in Yaroslavi. I really miss you a lot but I know you need some time there to renew some old acquaintances. Just hope some beautiful woman didn't catch your eye. Everything is running smoothly here and Sergey deserves a lot of credit for finding and hiring Dmitry Cherkin. He is not only well qualified in every respect but has a natural ability to neutralize a potential problem. Along with his great personality he is not bad looking either. It is a wonder that one of the girls at the office hasn't made a move on him yet. Of course, I don't know what his marital status is. Anyway, I can't wait for your return on Thursday. I will pick you up at the airport at 3pm. Love you, Lana."

Vasily could only smile when he read the note because he interpreted the part about Dmitry as an attempt to make him jealous. In fact, he felt a little relieved because although he cared very much for Lana, in his heart, he understood the difference in age between them presented a formidable obstacle to any future union. He remembered seeing Dmitry's age on his application form as being 34. Lana was approaching 27 so this was a potential good match. He would wait until morning to write back because the gin tonic had worked it's magic and soon he was in the land of dreams.

The next morning he felt refreshed and invigorated. The visit to see Radinka and Jacob Novokov had taken much off his mind regarding their feelings toward him, especially when Radinka learned he was the father of her future grandchild. In less than a year his tenure at the new facility in Sverdlovsk would end and he could begin to think of perhaps finally being able to travel to places he once envisioned.

Yes the trip to Delmarva to be with Olga, her daughters, and new husband Judge Walker, took his mind off of losing Yelena and with a home now in Chincoteague he would go back to visit one day but he also wanted to see some of the cities in Western Europe such as Rome, Berlin, Munich, Zurich, as well as a desire to return to Paris and London. He would love to take Lana with him on some of those excursions but her responsibilities at the Sverdlovsk facility would afford her scant time to travel, at least, for the first couple of years.

A Delightful Surprise at the Breakfast Diner

It was now Tuesday morning and he had just several more days on his one week break before returning to Sverdlovsk. Vasily fired an e-mail off to Lana telling her how much he missed her and would be looking forward to seeing her at the airport on Thursday afternoon. But he was feeling buoyant and didn't want to waste one hour of his time so he went down to the diner to have breakfast. It was a little late and most of the old timers that frequented the place would probably already be gone, but at least he could say hello to some of the help and have his favorite Russian pancakes, and grits.

When he entered he heard a woman's voice from the far corner, "Hi Vasily, I would be quite honored if you would join me for breakfast." He looked over his shoulder and noticed a strikingly good looking woman sitting at a table with a newspaper in her hand. Her face was familiar but her name escaped him for a moment. Of course it was Polina Botkina. They had met several years back at the Radisson Hotel for dinner. She was the RIS operative who supervised his father Bill Bond during his incarceration in Chelyabinsk many years earlier. Vasily was almost speechless but he managed a few words by accepting her invitation, "I can't think of anyone I would rather be with for breakfast or any other occasion."

They hugged as if they were long time acquaintances and since she spent 14 months with his father several decades earlier one might consider they had a natural bond. She must be about 50 now and she was spectacular. Very trim, with a smooth attractive tanned face, and beguiling smile, she was quite a desirable woman and Vasily was anxious to learn more about her life. He remembered when they last met she told him she had married when she was young to a fellow RIS graduate Alex who died in a boat accident but she had never married again.

Polina explained that she was in Yaroslavi to investigate a minor airplane accident to be sure it had nothing to do with any kind of terrorist activity. She had several days remaining here to conclude her investigation before going back to Moscow. Of course that could only mean she was still working as a RIS operative. They must have talked at least an hour and Polina spent most of that time reminiscing about the time she and Bill Bond spent together in Chelyabinsk many years ago. "And by the way, Vasily, I remember when you and I had dinner at The Radisson you told me you were an amateur masseur and invited me to your suite for a massage free of charge. I couldn't accept at that time but I am available if you have time over the next few days." Vasily quickly thought about Lana and possible repercussions but after his offer to her at the Radisson he felt compelled to respond, "Of course I would be most happy to provide you with my services. Where are you staying?" She responded; "The Saint George Hotel on Moskovskiy Prospkt."

"In that case, may I make a suggestion, why don't you check out of the hotel this afternoon? I will pick you up there at 2 p.m and we can go to my home where I have all the necessary equipment to make your massage a more enjoyable experience. After that, you can enjoy my hot tub, and with your permission I will be happy to dry you off with a special Turkish towel, and before we proceed to dinner. When we return later, I can provide you with another version of my services, before you retire for the evening. When you awake the next morning I will make your breakfast." After his offer she gave him an agreeable smile before responding, "Mr. Sokolov, you have made me an offer I can't refuse."

After their breakfast at the diner she wanted to walk the short distance to her hotel for the exercise and said she would eagerly await his arrival at 2 p.m. Vasily could not believe his good fortune since arriving in Yaroslavi just five days ago. Meeting with Radinka and Jacob Novokov, finding out that Sergey and Darya would be tying the knot soon, and now his conversation with Polina Botkina and the anticipation of what might follow this evening. He immediately went home to prepare for his afternoon guest. Just as he had done for Olga at the Ecotel many years earlier he made a makeshift tanning bed on the floor of the master bedroom suite. He checked to be certain the hot tub was in good working order and would wait patiently until 1:45 p.m when he would meet Polina at the St. George Hotel.

When Vasily got there, she was waiting in the lobby with her piece of luggage. They hugged and on the way to his home she moved her hand to his right thigh while giving him the sexy smile he remembered earlier at breakfast. If this was part of the deal he was in no position to refuse because his heart was beating quickly and he was feeling the effects.

When they arrived at his home he went to the refrigerator to offer her a drink. She wanted a beer and as he showed her around his home their tour ended in the master bedroom suite when she noticed the makeshift bed. She requested that he remove her clothing one piece at the time while she was removing his in alternating fashion. If this was a fantasy thing with her or something she experienced with someone else it didn't matter.

When Vasily removed her last piece of lingerie it was as if someone of great skill had sculptured her body from a huge piece of clay. Her breasts were round and firm, her torso and thighs blending together like a perfect Vermeer masterpiece. While his eyes feasted on this 50 year old specimen of womanhood he placed his hand on her shoulder and turned her 180 degrees. Except for a small birthmark on her upper right buttock her skin was flawless.

When he turned her back around she understood he needed immediate relief so she gave him a hand massage and in a short time he achieved a full release. Maybe it reminded her of the time she and his father, Bill Bond, were doing the bolero some 25 years earlier. After cleaning things up she understood he needed recovery time so she insisted he lay down on the makeshift bed while she gave him a full body massage. Why she insisted on giving him relief and a massage first would only be conjecture on his part but the woman always sets the criteria, at least in his mind.

About 40 minutes later he returned the favor by first sprinkling some intoxicating oil over her entire body. Moving his hands slowly in a circular motion he moved slowly from her breasts to her vulva and thighs. He massaged her clitoris and vagina and she left no doubt that her long delayed massage was worth the wait. The sounds she made were an expression of satisfaction. They then walked to the hot tub where its warm circulating waters provided the perfect ending to a most enjoyable afternoon for both. As promised earlier, he took his soft Turkish towel and dried her off slowly before driving to the Hemingway Ale House where both enjoyed their sumptuous steaks and red merlot.

At this time Vasily became increasingly curious about her life beyond her job at the RIS. "I remember you told me you had married a fellow RIS graduate and after his sad demise and a long recovery period you continued your career and was assigned to Chelyabinsk. Do you feel comfortable in filling me in about your life over the ensuing several decades?"

His question seemed to catch her off guard so it took a moment to gather her thoughts. "I am sure you don't have the time or patience to listen to all that has happened to me over that period of time but maybe I can fill you in on some of it. I was 24 when I married Alex after our graduation from the RIS Academy and I believe no couple could possibly be more in love than we were. When you and I were at the Radisson I told you about the boat accident and his tragic death." At this time a tear came into her eye and Vasily took a tissue and wiped it away and then she continued; "Somehow I think I am repeating what I told your father all those years ago. After taking time off to see if I wanted to continue my career with the RIS I decided it was my only viable option, and I was assigned to Chelyabinsk to supervise your father's incarceration. He was the perfect antidote for my despondency because even though he was being held on trumped up charges, without being able to contact his loved ones, his spirit remained high."

"Your father was decades older than me but after about eight months into his 14 month stay I found myself falling in love with him. It wasn't the kind of love I shared with Alex but something far more complicated. I knew he was in love with a 40 year old woman from St. Petersburg and until our Ravel bolero there was never a hint of any sexual involvement between us. I am sure his desire to share a bed during our time together was as strong as mine but we never let it happen." At this time she took a sip of merlot and said she would wait until they got back to his home to continue, since they were the only two remaining at Hemingway's, and the manager was anxious to close.

When they opened the door to Vasily's home they got into some comfortable garments and sat in the kitchen where she completed her thoughts. "Anyway, when I took your father to the train depot after he had gained his freedom and waved goodbye to him as his train pulled away I didn't know how I could live without him. I had many varying assignments after my 14 month stay at Chelyabinsk but after first losing Alex and then not having Bill Bond to get me through the tough emotional times I became reclusive almost like a nun." As the years passed I met some really nice gentlemen but never felt the intensity required to think about marriage or even a serious relationship. Well Vasily, I hope I didn't bore you."

With that, Vasily got off his chair and put his arms around her and knowing it was getting late after their long day he finally was able to speak. "I know you are tired so why don't we retire for this evening. Would you consider sharing a bed with me?" It took her a few seconds to respond, "Yes, but only if we are in the nude. I need your body next to mine more than you will ever know."

With that, they retreated to the master bedroom hand in hand. It was as if they were newlyweds because their emotions had taken over as their lips joined as one and within minutes he was under her spell doing all the things she was requesting, not so much with her voice but the movement of her body. Her nipples moved to his lips in alternating ways allowing him enough time to savor each one while she guided his hand to her vulva and upper thighs. It was strange in a way because they were so anxious to be in bed together they decided to forgo the second massage.

It was a night that neither wanted to end but when morning arrived reality began to sink in for both of them. This would be their last day together because tomorrow morning she would be boarding a train to take her to Moscow while he took a plane back to Sverdlovsk.

Both knew that somehow they would meet again in the future but because of complications in their lives they couldn't make any near term arrangements. They would keep in touch through electronic mail until an ideal opportunity presented itself. After Vasily prepared the breakfast he had promised the night before, they spent the remainder of the day in the hot tub and bed not wanting to lose the momentum from the day and night before. Later that evening, they had Chinese food delivered from the Chen Fen carryout right down the road which seemed a little strange in a Russian city like Yaroslavi, but this type of food fit their appetites perfectly. As the hours began to tick off way too quickly and as night turned into morning their glorious two days was ending. He drove her to the train station and it was like the reverse of what she described when she took Bill Bond to the depot in Chelyabinsk so many years ago. This time after their final hug he waved goodbye as she boarded the train to Moscow.

In three hours his plane would depart for Sverdlovsk so he drove the company van to the old facility where he would spend some time with Sergey Petrov and Darya Alfyorova as well as some old employees he missed so much. After his visit there, Darya drove him to the airport and she broke the news that she and Sergey would be married in July of next year although the actual day and place had not yet been set. She thanked Vasily for giving her a job at a time when her life was in turmoil and now she had everything she ever wanted in life. Yes, Nada and Pavel were not her birth children but she loved them and they learned to respect her after the demise of their mother Yelena Petrova.

When Darya left him off at the terminal they hugged tightly not in a way that would suggest any romance between them but instead out of deep respect for what they had achieved and endured together over the past decade. As far as Vasily knew Darya had no knowledge about the relationship he and Yelena shared or the circumstances of Yelena's pregnancy.

During his flight back to Sverdlovsk he understood his life was becoming more complicated than he ever envisioned. Although he had met Polina Botkina at the Radisson Hotel in Moscow for dinner several years earlier he never could imagine her re-entering his life in such a profound way.

With Lana meeting him in just an hour at the Koltsova terminal he was well aware of the possible implications in their relationship if he found it necessary to tell her about Ms. Botkina. Lana was 26 and Polina was fifty but despite their age difference there was a warmness and kindness they both possessed in good measure. If he had to choose between them in some future proposal to marry it would be an almost impossible decision for him to make.

Although over two years had gone by since Yelena's dreadful accident and thinking of marrying anyone else was still too difficult to contemplate. The intensity of their love for each other could not be measured in strictly earthly terms. His out of body experience on the hillside where he was reunited with her and their new born son Jacob, could never be erased or forgotten regardless of what the future might bring.

When he landed at Koltsova Lana was waiting and they drove straight to the office to discuss all that had transpired in the past week. There were a few minor problems in the field but with the number of jobs and contracts the company was undertaking this was not unexpected. Dmitry Cherkin had proved to be the perfect person to settle any misunderstanding between the company and their customers. Since Vasily stressed both integrity and fairness from the beginning, the Sokolov Cement and Concrete Corporation both here, and Yaroslavi, would never sacrifice those tenets.

For the next several months Vasily and Lana resumed their close relationship both on the social front and in the bedroom while Vasily wrote almost daily to Polina Botkina. The summer was ending and the nip of autumn was in the air when Vasily decided to visit a huge highway expansion project near Chelyabinsk.

The facility now had 30 concrete delivery trucks and ten of them were traveling back and forth on an hourly basis for this project alone. Vasily's foreman, for this particular project, Lionid Zubov, was doing an excellent job coordinating the various crews but Vasily wanted to be sure he had all the necessary manpower and Lionid assured him all bases were covered.

An Untimely Accident

It was almost dusk when Vasily headed back home for the 90 minute drive when the first snow of the season began. It was totally unexpected and the white stuff began to accumulate on the highway. When he approached a busy intersection the driver of a big 18 wheeler hit his brakes but before it could stop it slid into Vasily's van.

When the medics arrived Vasily was unconscious and when they moved him onto a stretcher it was obvious his injuries were serious so the doctor at the scene, called for a specially equipped helicopter, directing the pilot to go to the Marinsky Hospital in Moscow, where he knew there was a heliport and a special shock trauma unit. Yes, it was a long flight but the physician determined it was the victim's best chance for survival. When they arrived at the hospital, a medical team had been alerted in advance and they immediately began the testing. Yes, there were leg and body injuries that would eventually heal but it was the head injury that concerned them the most.

After several days in a coma-like condition the medical staff determined there were severe bruises on the left side of the brain that would eventually heal but they would have to keep him in an induced coma for up to 30 days and he would have to be fed intravenously for that period of time. His loved ones were notified but no one would be allowed to visit until his full recovery.

The Vision

{Editor's note;} (It is now time to digress from real life into the dream or vision that Vasily experienced during the time he was in his comatose state.)

Vasily was walking down a dark country road when he saw the flickering lights off in the distance. He ran and stumbled until he came upon a wood bridge traversing a small river whose ripples he could hear clearly now. The first half of the bridge was an incline that led to an apex that he imagined upon reaching would be a corresponding decline which would get him across the river to a place where the lights were emanating. As he walked up the incline the creaking boards of oak reminded him of an old bridge in his hometown that was constructed in the 17th century. As he approached the apex the lights became brighter and now he was near the top. Before walking the final few yards he stopped to think and began to wonder whether he should continue on or turn back. But if he turned back all that was there was a lonely dark country road so his choice was easy and when he got to the top he could not believe what he was witnessing on the other side.

A village town of lamp lights, horse and buggy's, log houses and people walking briskly in all directions as if they were on a mission of some sort. As he walked slowly down the decline he could now begin to hear their voices as they chatted with one another. Then he could not help but notice a woman almost in a trot with a small boy at her side coming on a path that would bring her to the bottom of the bridge. And then he heard her voice, "Oh Vasily, you are finally here, please hurry down, the bridge will disappear when the village clock strikes nine and we have waited so long to be with you again."

It was Yelena and as his walk turned into a run he could hear the oak boards from behind him falling into the river below. Would he be able to get to her in time or would he descend into the rushing waters. But just as the clock struck nine he rushed into her arms and she was real and they both could not let go as their tears began to flow. After a few minutes in tight embrace he heard the little boy at her side. "Mommy, mommy is this daddy?" "Yes, Jacob this is your father, he has not seen you since you were one day old on the hillside near Sverdlovsk. I had but a brief moment at that time and had to hurry back to the village before he could hold you but he is here now and we will be together forever. Vasily, pick him up and hold him, he needs your love." Needless to say Vasily was in a semi state of shock as he held the little boy in his arms and he could not believe his eyes as Jacob reminded him of a picture of himself when he was a young boy being held by his mother Galina.

"Come, I will take you to our little cabin. Give Jacob a piggy back ride and when we get home I have so much to tell you and tonight we will share our bed since I am anxious to begin a plan where Jacob will have several siblings in the future and I have already thought of some names." When they arrived at the cabin Vasily could not believe how small and cramped it was. He remembered how important the spacious kitchen and huge sewing room was to her in Yaroslavi and Sverdlovsk, and now she was reduced to this. He realized that this was a much earlier time in history but she wanted more children and this home was too small for even the three of them.

"I know what you are thinking Vasily but I have my eye on a farm outside the town where we can grow and build together. Now that you are here the authorities will be more receptive to our requests when we apply for a loan. As you can see our roads are nothing more than hardened earth and since you are an expert in road design and construction perhaps you can start your own company."

By this time Jacob began to ask some questions of his own. "Daddy, will you please take me to the river to fish tomorrow and can we go to see grandmother, Galina, and grandpa Vitali?" Vasily was stunned by this revelation when Yelena intervened, "Yes, I was going to tell you that your mom and dad are here living in a comfortable cabin just a few kilometers outside our village and my dad Jacob is now a part of our community just arriving several months ago."

Trying to get a grasp of everything he was hearing was too overwhelming to digest, when Yelena assured Jacob that eventually his daddy would take him fishing, and all the other places like visiting his grandparents and teaching him how to bait a hook, and kick a soccer ball as she tucked him into bed for the evening. Then she took Vasily by the hand and led him to a makeshift shower where she began to disrobe him piece by piece. As the refreshing stream ran over his body her hand movements were invigorating beyond description finally culminating with tender kisses to his most sensitive extremities.

"Now Vasily I want you to disrobe me in the same manner and when you are finished we will go to bed and try to make another baby. It is the right time of the month for me."

Her breasts were just as he remembered them and as he moved his lips to them and then downward to her vulva he thought this must be the paradise that the Greeks talked about in all the early writings by the great philosophers. Now seeing her lying in the nude on the small makeshift bed she asked him to prepare her properly and enter her vagina and begin the fertilization of the egg she knew was present in her womb. For the remainder of that night and all the days that followed, Vasily was the happiest he could ever remember. Being reunited with his mother Galina and stepfather Vitali, and now Yelena's father, Jacob was most special.

In the ensuing days he went to the bank to ask for a loan to purchase the farm and begin his road business. They were most receptive when they learned of his expertise. They explained that two young brothers were now running Russia and they were going to begin a major expansion of roads and bridges throughout all of Russia as well as building an entire new modern city on the Neva River near the Gulf of Finland in the north. The brothers implored all the banks in small towns and villages, to be vigilant in finding qualified people, to begin the planning and construction, with a central government guarantee that the funds would be available on a generous and timely basis.

And now Vasily knew the historical time frame he had been whisked into. The year had to be somewhere between 1682 and 1696 and the two brothers had to be Ivan the Fifth and his younger half-brother Peter. In the next four years Vasily and Yelena were now living on their farm with their two children, Jacob now age six and three year old Isidora. His road business was thriving and on many occasions Jacob and Isidora would get in the buggy and go with him to the various projects. Yelena would go with them on occasion but now with a big kitchen and spacious sewing room as well as a vegetable garden to attend to she was very happy to just be at home.

Things could not be going better, and with his mother Galina and Vitali, as well as her dad Jacob, visiting frequently, it was a family life every man would envy. He now had a contract to build a two lane road where two carriages could pass comfortably going in different directions. It would be almost 200 kilometers long and would connect their small village to a much bigger town called Samara. The specifications for the road project would be of Roman design that was first employed many hundreds of years earlier. First digging a three meter trench it would have four layers of thickness. The first being compacted soil, then a bedding of sand, followed by rows of flat stone and then covered with a slurry of gravel and lime. It was a monumental project requiring Vasily to hire 30 men along with all the necessary tools, horses and wagons. He hired his step father Vitali and father-in-law Jacob to be his foremen and both were more than eager to accept the challenge. The weeks went by quickly as the months turned into years and Vasily's reputation as a road builder was spreading across all of Russia. The road to Samara was completed under budget and ahead of schedule and after ten years of heavy carriage traffic it maintained its durability with minimal maintenance required.

Twenty years had passed since he had taken those final few steps into Yelena's arms and she was still as beautiful as he could ever remember. His family had grown from three to six as Alena and Peter joined Jacob and Isidora in the family ranks. With 18 year old Isidora and 15 year old Alena now home assisting Yelena with the canning, cooking and dressmaking and the two boys learning the road building business they were the perfect family. And Yelena was better than ever in the bedroom.

One early evening while having the family dinner a carriage pulled up in front with a young man in uniform delivering an envelope for Vasily. The messenger said he would return in less than a fortnight after his trip to Samara at which time he would pick up Vasily's response and deliver it to the Secretary of the Emperor. When he opened the envelope it contained this letter which he read to his family.

"Dear Mr. Sokolov: "It has come to our attention that you are the preeminent designer and builder of roads in all of Russia. The Emperor will be breaking ground on his visionary new city within the year and he will need your expertise. We will build the finest home in all of St. Petersburg for you and your family and will compensate you handsomely for your personal and business properties as well."

"Our messenger will be returning here in less than two fortnights, at which time we will expect nothing less than an enthusiastic response. The honors bestowed on you will be equal to those of the Emperor himself. On your property we will also build a four thousand square foot storage facility for your personal possessions, as well as a guest house to accommodate your family and friends."

Most Cordially Yours:

Peter the Great

When he completed reading the letter the family fell into complete silence which was in great contrast to their happy family conversations about their days activities and their plans for the future. Yelena's mother Radinka had recently come to the village which added to their happiness already abundant before her arrival but now they had to deal with a force that was totally unexpected but could not be ignored. It was at this time when Yelena stood up and addressed the family.

"Now we must shed our tears and face reality. It will be necessary for us to move to the new oblast because the Emperor is all powerful. We must look at the positive side only. Your dad has worked hard to achieve his sterling reputation and it will only be enhanced when we re-locate. Radinka, Galina, Vitali and Jacob will be able to visit us often and stay in the guest house as long as they wish. So now, let us finish our dinner and think only of a happy future in the new city that will be named St. Petersburg."

{Editor's Note.} (It is this time that Vasily awakens from his dream and comatose state in the intensive care unit at the Marinsky Hospital in Moscow.)

The bruises on his brain had healed several days earlier but because he was fighting against returning to reality his recovery would take a longer time. He was now peering up to a doctor and a woman dressed in a white uniform at which time she began to speak.

"Now Mr. Sokolov I will first ask you a number of questions to be sure you understand me."

At this time she began what the medical team called the testing phase to be sure he would fully understand all the information he would be receiving over the several weeks he would be here. After her bevy of questions which he apparently answered in a very satisfactory way she continued.

"Thirty four days ago you were involved in an accident when the van you were driving was hit broadside by an eighteen-wheeler. The driver received no injury but you were not as fortunate. You were treated for some relative minor injuries by the medical team at the scene but because you were in an unconscious state you were flown here for evaluation and treatment."

"When we did a head scan it showed no permanent damage but there were some rather severe bruises on the cerebellum, hypothalamus and corpus callosum sections of the brain. We have seen these types of bruises many times in the past and although they are not permanent they do require the patient to be immobile and quiet over a period of time which in your case required 34 days. We put you in an induced coma until your bruises were completely healed and I am happy to say that you are now ready to begin the next phase of your recovery."

"Over the past month you have been fed intravenously so as of today you will receive more solid food and in just two days you will begin an exercise program and in five days you will get a computer to access your personal and business e-mails which I am sure will keep you busy for quite a while."

"In ten days you will be allowed visitors and in two weeks you will be released from here and it is our hope you will not try to rush into your business and personal affairs too quickly. When I say affairs maybe you consider the word to have a double meaning but if you have that special woman in your life your love making can resume immediately after your release from here. As a matter of fact, getting your blood moving to all your vital parts will actually improve your equilibrium immensely."

"That is all from me for now but you will be assigned an attendant and trainer to get your diet and exercise routines started and I will check in with you in several days to see how you are progressing."

Now here alone in his thoughts he well understood that this dream or time warp he had experienced was something so much more. He had been thrust into the late 17th and early 18th century at the time of Peter the Great in some remote Russian village where he was reunited with Yelena and Jacob and their three added children, Isidora, Peter and Alena. He never wanted to leave their world but now he knew they would always be together no matter what transpired in the real world.

After a few days on a diet and exercise routine they provided him with a computer and as he perused his e-mails the memories began to return. This one was from Lana Matviyenko:

"Dear Vasily, we have learned you will have a complete recovery and I understand you can`t rush the process but I will be so happy when we can resume our life together as it was prior to your unfortunate accident. I understand our lovemaking will require patience on my part but I will look forward to leading you slowly to some exciting experiences in the future. I love you very much. Lana"

Then this one from Polina Botkina:

"Dear Vasily, I was so saddened when I heard of your accident. Our two days together at your house in Yaroslavi was unforgettable and

when your health is back to normal I hope we can resume some of the
activities and fun we enjoyed in your bedroom and hot tub. I would
even consider a more permanent arrangement if you think I am worthy.
Sincerely, Polina"

From Dasha Brumel: "Dear Vasily, I heard about your dreadful
mishap from my good friend Polina Botkina. She informed me you
will have a complete recovery. She made it sound as if she was going to
make a serious effort to make your relationship a more permanent one.
I didn't realize you were still in play or I would have given you more
to think about when you visited me in Paris. I will always have fond
memories of our visit to Versailles and of course in your suite at The
Four Seasons Hotel. The massage was super fantastic and the red roses
and bracelet only added to the ambiance. You are such a romantic guy.
If I thought I had even a little chance I am ready to offer Polina a little
competition." I am seriously yours. Dasha"

This one from Olga Kornakova:

"My Dear Vasily, I was greatly relieved when I learned your injuries
were not life threatening and your recovery will be complete. After
losing my husband Ben in such a traumatic way and discovering your
dad Bill Bond lying in his chair that morning I was not prepared
mentally for another shock. Judge Walker and I are doing fine and
my daughters have full time jobs in professions they thoroughly enjoy.
Maybe one day before long you will return to America and spend some
time in your Cape Cod at Chincoteague. You have always been very
special for me. Love, Olga."

There were many more letters from friends and associates like Svetlani
Cheranova reminding him that she wanted to complete the story of the
meteoric rise of the Sokolov Concrete and Cement Corporation now
that the Sverdlovsk facility was in operation. Also a nice letter from his
ex-wife Magdalina Brezhneva reminding him of the great times they
had in the past although she now regretted never having children.

Sergey Petrov and Darya Alfyorova wrote to say both branches of
the Sokolov Corporation were thriving and hugely profitable. They also
reminded him of their wedding next summer and both Pavel and Nada

were happy and doing well and were anxious to spend time with their Uncle Vasily after his full recovery.

In time he would answer all of them but after just five days out of his induced coma his mind could not release him into the real world because what he experienced while in his comatose state was too authentic, too real and in an attempt to understand this phenomenon he would need more time alone before reconnecting to all those he cared so much about. He had read scores of books by Sigmund Freud and others after his out of body experience on the hillside outside of Koltsova Airport. Some of the explanations he read about for this type of occurrence relieved his mind somewhat but what happened to him in this recent manifestation was so different that no book he read up to now could begin to explain how he was whisked into some 17th century Russian village where only those deceased in real life were present except for him, Radinka and the new born of that era were present.

Was it possible that Radinka Novokov had passed away while he was in his comatose state? If so, Sergey and Darya failed to mention this in their e-mail. As soon as he was released his first visit would be to Kostroma to see her. Vasily had called a Moscow dealership to order a heavy duty 8 wheel roadster (a fancy name for a heavy duty military type vehicle) a few days earlier and they would deliver the keys to him at the hospital in the morning. The next day he would depart the hospital, drive to his home in Yaroslavi and then to Kostroma and then on to Samara. But now it was time to write a general letter to everyone.

"My Dear Friends and Associates,

"By the time you receive this letter I will be traveling somewhere in Russia in my new 8 wheel drive roadster. Many of you will not understand why I didn't visit all of you who I care so much about immediately on my release. Some might believe I am not fully recovered and I am now in another phase of my recovery period. This is not the case as all my medical caretakers have pronounced me fit as a fiddle and quite able to perform any task or duty I was engaged in before my accident."

"I know that both divisions of the Sokolov Cement and Concrete Corporation are in good hands and besides it is now time for me to retire since that was my intention when I recruited Sergey Petrov. For lack of a better reason to describe my future travels just call it a mission to gain knowledge and get a better understanding of this planet we all inhabit. I can`t say how long I will be gone except to say I will return when I have found some answers to some issues I consider not only important to me but vital to those I care so much about. I love all of you. Sincerely, Vasily."

The morning of his release had now arrived and the medical staff came in to give him their handshakes and best wishes. On the drive from Moscow to Yaroslavi he knew he could not resume his life prior to where it was before the accident. He understood at some point in the future his relationships with Lana Matviyenko and Polina Botkina would need his full attention. It would not be fair to either to suggest a future until he could make some sense of what transpired in that remote Russian village from about 1690 to 1710 AD.

It was a cold winter day when he stopped at his house in Yaroslavi to pick up some winter clothing and gear for his journey ahead. Although the Sokolov facility was just a few miles up the road he decided not to visit for fear of having to explain to Sergey and Darya his mission which at this stage was unexplainable. So after checking to be sure his heating system with all the redundant backups were working well he got back in his roadster and headed for Kostroma.

When he arrived at the home where he had last spoken to Yelena`s mother Radinka Novokova snow had accumulated on the porch and there was little sign of foot prints. He knocked at the door but got no answer when a lady approached him from the sidewalk.

"My name is Nina Orlova and I was a good friend of Radinka`s until her passing about a month ago."

It was if Vasily`s tongue had been frozen because he could hardly speak but finally he responded.

"How could this be, I just visited her less than a year ago and she was healthy and in good spirit."

"When her husband Jacob passed she seemed to have lost her will to live. In fact, she told me of visions she had of Jacob and Yelena asking her to join them in their wonderful village. Kind of weird I thought but now I wonder. You probably are aware how she lost her beautiful daughter Yelena in that terrible plane accident near Sverdlovsk. She was pregnant at the time. Anyway, they are probably all together now."

Vasily, now holding back the tears thanked her and got back into his roadster and now he knew that what he experienced while in his comatose state was something so real that not even the most advanced studies could describe this phenomenon but somehow he needed to find some answers as he studied the road map because getting to Samara was the starting point if there was any hope of resolving his purgatorial experience. For lack of a better word to describe his apparition he would just call it his vision.

On the Road to Samara

In his visionary state he was a road builder which was similar to his real life as a government employee and owner of the Sokolov Concrete Company. The road he built from his village to Samara was engineered to last several hundred years and maybe he could find some remnant even though almost 350 years had gone by. It was the time of Peter the Great and although Peter was a young boy at the time he wanted a modern road system that would connect the new city he planned to build on the Neva River to the Caspian Sea. It would eventually be a 1500 kilometer road with 8 sections of about 200 kilometers. That was the length of road he built while a contractor in his vision. He now knew he could find the location of his village by plotting the obvious path from Samara to St. Petersburg. It would by-pass Moscow to the east.

The 625 mile trip from Kostroma to Samara took him through Nizhny Novgorod and Kazan and although the weather was a challenge at times, his roadster was built to handle slippery roads so after a few stops he was in Samara in a little over 12 hours. He immediately checked into a two room suite at the Azimut Hotel for 2 weeks. He had the option of extending if necessary. They were known for their comfortable accommodations and hearty breakfast buffets and since his days on the road would be long a good breakfast was essential.

Vasily wasted little time and after a restful night in their king sized feathered bed he was ready to go to work and his first visits would be to the various libraries to get a history lesson on this most interesting city. Viewing some of the early pictures of the city it was in deep contrast to what he was seeing today. A modern Metropolis of over a million people located at the fork of the Volga and Samara rivers, today's faces on the streets and buses were ones of both hope and concern.

Although the official start of the city was in 1586 when a fortress was built to protect the region from wondering nomads intent on plundering and pillaging everything that others had built, it wasn't until 1600 when the first custom offices were established. The period of time he was most interested in was the years between 1690 and 1710 which covered the twenty years of his vision. He estimated there were probably about twenty thousand inhabitants residing there in various types of structures including river huts and small houses of wood. The maps of the early roads in the region were mostly post 1725 and the ones today were almost exclusively concrete or black top so finding the remnants of the old section he both engineered and constructed during his vision around 1695 to 1702 would be a challenge. Fortunately for him, being a graduate of the Moscow State University Engineering School and being the owner and operator of the Sokolov Corporation he understood the business well.

For the next week he plotted the route from Samara to St. Petersburg using the existing highways as the place to start because most likely the new roads were built over the older ones over the last three and a half centuries. He received permission from the authorities to bore six holes in three different locations 4 inches in diameter 10 meters deep on the existing roads explaining to them he was on a historical mission of great importance. He hired a local contractor to both bore the holes and fill them in immediately after collecting the core samples.

His first two bore holes would be in an area where he plotted by triangulation would be the end of the old road in Samara. The first bore sample was not helpful but the second one just 400 meters in the direction of where the old village would have been located hit pay dirt so to speak, and now he knew it was not just a vision he experienced but something so real it could not be denied or refuted by anyone. On the 10 meters deep core sample the first 6 meters gave us the history over the past 250 years of road construction but from 6 meters through 9 meters mark represented the 100 years prior and it told Vasily everything he wanted to know. Four distinct layers of gravel and lime slurry, stone, sand and compacted soil which were the exact specifications of his early road near the end of the 17th century.

His next four bore holes near the end of the 200 kilometers told him exactly where the old road ended but now there was no village. Except for the road itself it was nothing more than a heavy forested area. But how could this be? 350 years ago it was a thriving village. Within several kilometers of where he was now standing he was so deliriously happy living with Yelena and his four children Jacob, Isidora, Alena and Peter three of which were born here with the help of his mother Galina who lived a short distance down the road with his step father Vitali. Of course Jacob was no doubt born here but that was before he arrived.

In his own mind he had all the convincing evidence that some part of him at another time lived here but now he wanted further clarification beyond the road cores and the death of Radinka Novokova while he was lying in some twilight zone at the Marinsky Hospital in Moscow.

Oak Saplings and a Bell

It was a cold December night when he entered the hot tub at the Azimut Hotel when something jogged his memory. During his time in that village some three and a half centuries ago he remembered a short bearded man everyone called the Tree Man. In that period of time while Vasily and his crew were constructing the very road where he had collected the road cores the Tree Man would come out of the forest during their breaks and give everyone a lesson on how to determine the age of various trees in the immediate vicinity of where they were working. In particular, he pointed out two giant indigenous oak trees he claimed were over 500 years old. If he was right it would have meant their vintage would have been sometime in the 12th century AD. He had a collection of small saplings he was selling at a bargain price and Vasily bought a dozen of them.

In a kidding way Vasily asked if he would guarantee they would live for 500 years. Vasily remembered planting all twelve on the east perimeter of his property exactly 22 meters apart near a water well. He watered the saplings regularly until their roots were well developed and for sure they got off to a good start. He would lower the big bucket with a cast iron bell as an anchor nearly thirty meters on a sailors rope and then water each one using about a quarter of a bucket on each.

He couldn't wait until the next day to take the 3 hour drive back and his mission would be to find some clue regarding the twelve saplings and just how long they may have survived. He got out of the hot tub and dried off and after dressing went to the hotel bar for a gin and tonic. He set his alarm for 5am because he wanted their great buffet breakfast before driving the 200 kilometers where he would begin his detective work.

The great thing about his military style roadster, there was plenty of space for survival gear and on his way here to Samara he stopped in Kazan to purchase a propane generator, 4 drums of propane, a tent, an electric heater, a heavy duty sleeping bag, wool blankets, flares, canned rations, along with the latest compass and map system that would guide him out of the forest if necessary.

It was 6am when he got on the road toward the old village and he was as excited as he could ever remember. He took his off the road vehicle as far as he could into the forest before setting up camp. It was -10 C when he departed Samara and he was the only one in the area. Russians are a hearty breed but if hunters were around he saw no one nor could he hear the sound of their trusty hunting rifles crackling in the morning fog.

After setting up his tent he checked his generator and it was working fine. The small heater kept the inside of his tent toasty warm. But its comfort would be for later because it was now time to set out on foot to search for any evidence of the 12 oak trees he had planted as saplings three and half centuries earlier.

He carried a collection of machetes to get through some of the heavier undergrowth and he put red duct tape strips on a tree about 25 meters apart marking each strip with a black marker with a number corresponding to his advancement into the forest. He knew from the road core and the small river going through the area that his tent was sitting where the center of the old village was once located. The farm and property where he, Yelena and their four children spent twenty happy years from 1690 to 1710 was located about 4 kilometers northeast of his tent location if his calculations were right.

But hiking through 4 kilometers of underbrush was a formidable task and although the trip back would be easier he set 3pm as the time to head back to his tent. He had left his tent at 930 am and now at 2:30 pm he was in the area where he thought he had planted his saplings all those centuries ago. He was dead tired so he sat down on an old tree stump to have a few food rations knowing his time to head back was just 30 minutes away. And then a strange thought entered his mind. What if the very stump he was sitting on was the remnant of one of those oak saplings?

Without thinking he jumped off the stump and counted the markings. This kind of science was not his expertise but if his ring counts were anywhere near correct it had lived for three hundred years and had been cut down just fifty years before. He immediately took his measuring tape and began to clear a path and then at 22 meters there was another stump with the same amount of markings and now he knew he had found the perimeter of his old farm and property. Of course he understood he would need to return over the ensuing days to find evidence for the remaining trees but he was confident his discovery was the confirmation he needed to continue his search. His excitement could not be contained as his emotions began to overwhelm the careful plan he had mapped for himself.

It was 5:30 pm when he got back to his tent but instead of spending the night here he decided to do the three hour drive back to Samara since he would need to contact a contractor there in the morning anyhow. Besides, sleeping in a warm king sized bed made more sense than hunkering down in a sleeping bag inside his tent. So he took down his tent and gathered his survival gear and arrived at the Azimut Hotel at 9pm.

He was so elated he decided to take a hot shower and go down to the hotel bar for a nightcap. A strikingly beautiful lady of the night came over and sat next to him. She introduced herself as Tasha Zabova and it didn't take her long to begin a conversation.

"I am not going to ask you to go to bed with me because you look so happy and my job is to lift the spirit of those who are a little down on their luck. Until that person shows up I would love to talk to you so if you can afford to buy me a drink I will be happy to keep you company."

She was wearing an outfit that revealed all her god given assets and she seemed intent on giving him a good look of her perfect breasts which reminded him of Lana Matviyenko. Sex was not on his mind when he began his mission after being released from the Marinsky Hospital in Moscow. She looked to be about 25 and although he had no intention of taking her to his suite she became a very interesting person and conversationalist.

He remembered the story that Arno, his guide and taxi driver in St. Petersburg related to him on how his biological father Bill Bond had met a lady of the night by the name of Vera Petrova and would have married her had she not perished in an accident. The same Vera Petrova was the mother of Sergey Petrov who he hired as CEO for his concrete business. And of course Sergey was the husband of Yelena, the woman he fell in love with from the first moment he laid eyes on her.

They were now on their third drink when her hand moved to his groin area at which time he took her by the hand and led her to his suite. What happened that night between them would not be important because he recognized that she was a very smart and talented young woman with the possibility of being a future leader in industry. Vasily wanted to give her every opportunity by offering to pay for her education and getting a job for her while she attended school. When he drove her to her flat the next morning he knew another woman was now a part of his real life. Tasha Zabova had made a deep impression on him and they agreed to meet again to discuss her future before he left Samara.

But now it was time to find a contractor that would accompany him back to the area of the two oak tree stumps. What he was most interested in was locating the old water well he used to hoist the water for the saplings back those many years ago. The cast iron bell he used to anchor his water bucket had fallen off and maybe by some miracle they could retrieve it. Instead of using a contractor to clear the area since it would take many permits from local officials he decided to find a single owner well digger willing to move his gear into the forest. After a day of searching he found just the person he was looking for.

A big burly man by the name Lucifer with hair covering his entire body, he looked forward to the challenge providing the pay was good and a bonus was in store if they found the well and recovered the cast iron bell which bore the initials of the Hemony brothers with the year

1661 emblazoned on the outer sheave. Vasily remembered purchasing the bell from the local village blacksmith without having any real reason for doing so, which he eventually used for an anchor tied to the bottom of his water bucket.

It was now Tuesday and Lucifer agreed to move his equipment to the site on Friday, and this would give Vasily Wednesday and Thursday to go back with his survival gear in an attempt to locate the remaining oak tree stumps and once doing so he could almost pinpoint the location of the old well.

On Tuesday evening he met again with Tasha Zubova and when he told her he would be living and sleeping in a tent on the edge of a forest for several days she begged him to let her go along. She was an accomplished skier and her outer wear was well suited for the extreme outdoor climate. At first he turned her down but she was insistent and like most beautiful ladies in his past he succumbed to her charm and besides having her to snuggle up with anywhere was not such a bad thing.

Of course he could not divulge to her that he lived in that village 350 years earlier so he gave her the same story he gave to Lucifer claiming he had found a document that traced his heritage back 14 generations to a small Russian village that once thrived there. This peaked Tasha's interest even more and she agreed to stay with Vasily in his suite this evening because they would have an early 6AM departure time in the morning. So after going over to her flat to pick up her gear and heavy clothing they had a drink at the hotel and took a hot shower together in his suite and then settled in for the night.

The next morning Tasha was so anxious to get started she actually got up before the 5am alarm went off and after removing the blankets from his body began to use her hand and fingers to massage his thighs and groin area, "I am going to give you something before you get up because you have made me feel as if I am a very special woman."

It was quite a wakeup call as both he and the alarm went off at the very same moment. After their morning shower and breakfast they were on the road and after a lengthy conversation about her future they arrived at the place where Vasily had set up his tent several days earlier. After putting up their tent and getting dressed for the frigid temperatures Tasha chose a machete from his collection and now they were on their way back to the site of the two oak tree stumps. Since Vasily had cleared a path and marked the trail when he was here several days earlier the 4 kilometer hike would be much quicker and when they arrived in 90 minutes they went right to work.

Tasha was a real trooper as she and Vasily began to clear the underbrush to where he calculated would be the next tree stump. And now after two days of hard work and hiking back and forth to and from their camp area they had discovered 6 more well-preserved stumps now making a total of 8. But what happened to the remaining two? They couldn't see the forest for the trees because 22 meters from the two end stumps stood two giant oak trees. Those who harvested the eight decided to let two of them remaining and now they were feasting their eyes on two magnificent goliaths now nearly 350 years old.

Vasily thought back to the Tree Man who told him the young saplings he purchased would live for 500 years or more and observing how healthy and vigorous they appeared who could deny that they wouldn't be here 150 years from now. It was now late Thursday afternoon and Vasily measured off a 20 meter square area where he thought the well might be. Lucifer would be here in the morning with all his equipment and the job of digging and clearing would be left for him.

Vasily and Tasha were tired warriors when they retired to their tent for the evening. The propane generator outside their tent with its gentle hum was designed to keep predators away and the little electric heater kept their tent cozy warm as they cuddled up for the long winter night. When he looked at Tasha's face it was dirty with a small scratch across her chin. He took a warm, wet cloth he had placed near the heater and began to wipe her face and chin and she began to smile. She was more beautiful than ever as they kissed and hugged before going sound asleep after a most grueling but productive day.

When they awoke it was Friday morning and Lucifer would be here in approximately two hours. They opened their ration cans and ate the pasta-like sustenance they had been using since they arrived. No matter what happened today they vowed to drive back to the Azimut Hotel tonight and enjoy all the amenities they offered.

There was no mistaking the sound of the piece of equipment Lucifer was driving when he pulled up to their tent.

"Hop on the front and direct me to the area you want me to explore."

It was like getting a command from an infantry general and Tasha and Vasily wasted little time in jumping to his order and soon they were heading for the perimeter of his 350 year old farm. Lucifer immediately attached a huge shovel to the long extended arm of his tractor and soon he was removing huge slabs of debris, growth and dirt and setting them aside. After just 3 hours he hit a huge slab of concrete.

Lucifer seemed excited when he proclaimed, "Underneath that slab will be the well you wanted to find. I have run into this type of seal in the past. When loggers have completed their harvest in a particular hectare they seal them in such a way that succeeding generations can use them since these wells never run dry being fed by underground aquifers."

Vasily could not believe what he was hearing as Lucifer removed the shovel he was using and replaced it with another shovel more suitable for getting under the slab and lifting it off. After removing the slab he gently removed about 2 meters of earth and then there it was, a round one half meter terra cotta lining with another smaller slab on top. After removing the smaller slab Lucifer peered down into the opening and hollered.

"Hey down there, we have come to get your treasures and I have a special message for you Madame Bell. If you are down there I will find you because Mr. Sokolov has promised me a handsome bonus if I can bring you to the top."

Of course when he referred to Madame Bell he was talking about the bell he used as an anchor on the bottom of his water bucket. Lucifer was as excited and anxious as Vasily at the prospect of uncovering a three and a half century hidden relic as he began to assemble his ropes and pulleys for the next phase of the operation. He lowered his first rope and anchor to where he heard the first splash of water. He then lowered it until it hit bottom and now he knew the water was four meters deep.

Now it was time to use his hydraulic lift fitting a claw-like device on it that could be opened or closed with a pedal he attached to the lift with a hose filled with hydraulic fluid. Tasha had hardly spoken a word during the entire operation seeming mesmerized by what she was watching. Lucifer was now lowering his claw-like device and for the first hour all he retrieved was sediment and dirt. Then after a while longer stone and pieces of old bucket began to appear. At the 3 hour mark he retrieved a rusted piece of cast iron and laid it at Vasily's feet.

"THERE MR. VASILY IS YOUR PRECIOUS BELL. IT WILL TAKE SOME CLEANING UP FROM A METALLURGIST BUT AFTER SOME TIME IT WILL BE JUST LIKE THE WAY YOUR 14TH GENERATION RELATIVE LEFT IT."

Although the markings were not visible he was as confident as Lucifer that this was the final piece of the puzzle. There was now no doubt that he had lived here with Yelena and his children for 20 years from 1690 to 1710. He put his arms around Tasha and hugged her tightly, and then rushed over to Lucifer and put his arm around this hairy giant of a man he had just met earlier in the week.

He was happy beyond his most vivid imagination and he wanted to celebrate. It was 3pm and Lucifer needed several more hours to put everything back as closely as they had found it. After they had finished they climbed back on Lucifer's tractor with their treasured piece of cast iron when Vasily asked Lucifer to take them where he had parked his roadster. He went underneath it where he had stored two bags of gold coins he had put there in advance. He counted out enough to cover Lucifer's pay and bonus adding a few extra coins so that Lucifer could have a separate celebration with his friends and family because tomorrow was Saturday and nobody can celebrate better than Russian working men. They hugged once more before Lucifer drove off and now it was time for Tasha and Vasily to take down their tent and load up for the trip back to Samara.

After a weekend of joyous celebration with Tasha he wasted little time getting his precious piece of cast iron to the metallurgist Lucifer mentioned. After explaining the process to Vasily of what steps would be taken to bring it back to its 17th century condition he was told he could pick it up in 3 days.

While waiting he spent almost his entire time with Tasha Zabova. He wanted to be sure she had a chance for a rewarding and secure future. If she was willing to move to Moscow she could work at the Sokolov plans and specifications office and attend school at Moscow State University and he would supply the necessary funds until she was well established. If she decided to pursue an opportunity here in Samara he would provide the funds for whatever endeavor she chose providing she was willing to give up her life as "a lady of the night." And then she made a statement that would complicate his life for a long time.

"Vasily, I have known you for less than a fortnight but I love you more than you can imagine. I want to marry you and give you some children. Please say you will be my lover and mate and we will never part."

He knew her emotions were running high because after all how could either forget their time together during the search for the bell he coveted so much. Her dirty face he wiped with a damp cloth after a day of cutting underbrush with her machete would always be a precious memory. But the words she used although sincere were from a 25 year old woman who shared a bed with so many others over the past 4 years. There was little doubt that many of her clients mistreated her and now all of sudden she finds someone she respects and appreciates and falls deeply in love. And now it is up to Vasily to explain that it is necessary for her to wait at least a year to test the emotions she was now feeling and then they would discuss the possibilities for a future together.

After hearing his explanation on why they should wait she wept but like the trooper she was, she agreed it was probably the best for both of them. He left ample funds for her at the local bank until she decided whether to move to Moscow and take the job he offered her and attend school or stay in Samara and pursue a more worthwhile opportunity and giving up her life as a prostitute. Vasily was sure she would make the right decision.

The day had arrived to pick up his bell and when he saw it he was so emotional he wept because it was exactly as he remembered in his vision.

The year 1661 was emblazoned on the front with the Hemony Brothers insignia in small letters inside the sheave. Leonid, the metallurgist rang the bell and claimed it sounded just like it did those three and a half centuries earlier. He put in a special metal box and handed it to Vasily saying, "Mr. Sokolov you have a treasure worth a hundred times what you paid me to restore it. Take good care of it and put it under lock and key as soon as possible."

They shook hands and as Vasily loaded the box in a secret compartment he had installed under his roadster he began the long drive back to Kostroma and then on to Yaroslavi. His long drive back gave him time to reflect on all the things he would need to do when he got home. The women in his life would need to be handled in a special way because he had great affection and admiration for them all. He realized none could ever replace Yelena in both his earthly life and his visionary one but now nearing his middle 50's he would have some crucial decisions to make.

But that would be for another time and another book so stay tuned because you can bet Jac. K. Spence will be watching Vasily's every step and you can count on a thrilling and emotional high as you turn every page.

About the Book

"Yelena" is the follow-up novel to Jac. K. Spence's first book titled, "Bill and Olga." Vasily Sokolov, now forty three years of age learns from his dying Russian mother, Galina, that his biological father was an American by the name of Bill Bond, not Vitali Sokolov as he was led to believe. Vasily, a successful Russian bureaucrat, becomes a driven man as he sets out to learn all he can about his now deceased father. The journey he embarks upon leads him into situations so unimaginable and at times so sensual his ability to cope is severely tested.

About the Author

When my wife, Mary and I met a nice Russian lady at a local restaurant by the name of Katerina where she worked as a waitress we became instant friends. She invited us to visit her in Russia and we accepted her invitation without thinking twice about it. Our travels through this spectacular country with Katerina as our guide and interpreter was an unforgettable experience. The country and Katerina inspired me to pick up a pen and write a novel. My first book, titled, "Bill and Olga" was a lot of fun so I decided to follow up with "Yelena."